REALITY

OR

DREAM

WORLD

BY
Ruthie Shelton

First print

Published by
Ruthie Moore

Edited by
Missi Moore

Cover by
Jacob Thayer

International Standard Book Number (ISBN)
Paperback: 978-0-9862139-4-6
Printed in the United States of America
First print

Dedication

To my husband, James, you are my rock, my guiding light, and my strength. Thank you for always encouraging me to reach for my dreams.

To my children, Missi, J.C., Jenny, and Krystin, thank you for being proud of your mama. It means the world to me. I am so proud of all the goals each of you have reached. Keep learning and growing and stretching forward. The best days of your lives are still ahead!

Love you more!

Table of Contents

Chapter 1

"Lost but Found"

She slowly stretched her fingers out across the powdery soft sand she found herself lying on. With her eyes still closed, she could hear the waves crashing ashore. She licked her lips tasting the moist, salt air. As the tide came in, the cool water washed over her bare feet. She opened her eyes only to see rays of sunlight through her long, blonde, wet hair that draped across her face.

She raised herself up and crawled away from the incoming ocean. Feeling dazed and disoriented, she struggled to sit up. After taking a deep breath of fresh, revitalizing air, she looked around expecting to see other people.

To her surprise, there was no one. She looked to her left, then to her right. Miles and miles of beach was all she could see. In front of her was the endless horizon that the ocean offered. Behind her were only sand dunes and palm trees. As far as she could see in every direction, there was no one! This young woman was the only person on this deserted stretch of paradise or so she thought.

"How did I get here?" she thought to herself, "and where is 'here'?"

As she sat on that lonely beach, watching three pelicans dive for their supper, her senses were starting to come back to her.

"Magnolia!" she shouted. "That's my name! Magnolia," she said again quietly. "But why can't I remember anything else?"

After a long rest, she felt sturdy enough to stand up. As she got to her feet she brushed the sand off her hands. A warm evening breeze blew her sundress against her tanned legs.

Another wave washed ashore covering her feet with cool, clear water. Magnolia smiled and stretched as far as her arms would reach up.

She felt a sense of calmness and peacefulness come over her. "I don't know where I am or how I got here, but this place is BEAUTIFUL!" she said out loud, spinning around to look in all directions.

With a smile on her face and a dance in her step, she headed down the beach. She had no idea where she was going or what awaited her on that small strip of beach. She had no fear, no worries, no anxiety. But she also had no sense of time in this mystical place. All she knew was that she was seeing the most awesome site anyone had ever been privileged to witness.

The sun was dropping behind the dunes, and she wanted to catch every second of this sunset. She ran up the dunes to a group of palms and watched in awe as the sky put on a show just for her; at least that was how she viewed it. And what a show it was!

The colors were magnificent! Red, pink, orange and yellow, with swirls of white clouds against hues of blue and grey. As the red ball of fire slowly disappeared, the moon rose just in time to give Magnolia a brief glimpse of a light in the distance.

By this late hour this beach girl was getting hungry, thirsty, and extremely tired. She couldn't remember how she had gotten to that beach, so she had no idea what she had been through the last 24 hours. She just knew she felt exhausted and couldn't walk another step.

She dropped to her knees and leaned back against one of the palm trees. "I'll go see if I can find that light after I rest, for just a little while, I'll rest," she said to herself as her eyes fell shut.

Chapter 2

"City Life"

The sun was already bright in the sky when the alarm in the upstairs apartment started to ring. She covered her head with her pillow. It didn't quiet the sound of the ever louder shrieking of the alarm.

A muffled, "Ugh!" came from under the pillow. Then an arm slipped out from under the covers and slapped the clock... repeatedly. It took three or four good hits before the blaring noise stopped screaming at her; at least that's how she saw it.

She threw the pillow off her head and sat up in the bed. "No!" she screamed, "It can't be!" She looked around her bedroom to be sure she was really there. "I can't be back in my apartment," she cried, "it seemed so real. It couldn't have been just a dream!"

Just then she heard a banging on her door, "Come on Mags! Do you want to be late again?"

"Oh no! I have to get to work!" She ran to the door and let her best friend, Lisa, in.

"I have to tell you..." Mags started to say as she was running back to her bedroom to get dressed.

"Whatever it is can wait," Lisa said as she opened the refrigerator. "Hey, want some orange juice?" she yelled to her friend.

"No...well, yes. But I have to tell you about this dream," she said as she hopped into the kitchen with one shoe on and the other in her hand; all the while trying to put her hair up in a bun. "It was so real! I felt like I was there, on that beach!" She put her other shoe on and chugged down the juice.

Mags had thrown on the skirt she had worn the day before and a blouse that was hanging on the back of a chair, from who knows when, that wasn't tucked in yet.

Lisa, with every brown hair in place, make up always perfect, nails manicured and polished, wearing a two-piece suit and heels with matching purse, said, "Really Mags! Could you put a little more EFFORT into your appearance?"

Mags grabbed her extremely over-packed purse and said, "Didn't you say we needed to hurry?" changing the subject as she often did when she didn't want to discuss her bohemian lifestyle with her preppy friend.

Lisa was an executive assistant to the boss and felt that her presence in the office was vital to the success of the company, Monitek. Mags worked as a secretary, receptionist, file clerk or, as she often put it, a "do girl," "they tell me what to do and I do it."

As they walked, almost ran, down the stairs from her apartment, Mags tried to continue to tell her experience. "But I've never had a dream like this before. Not one that affected me this way. I'm sad that I'm not there on that beach. I want to go back."

Lisa pushed open the door to the 19th century Tudor style Brownstone home that had been converted into four apartments. "I am supposed to be in a meeting with the boss in three minutes. It takes ten minutes to walk to work from here. Can we just hoof it and talk about your dream later? Or is this another book you're writing? Never mind, we have to hurry!"

Lisa pointed to the open door with a look of exasperation on her face. Mags walked out of the apartment building still getting ready for work; tucking in her blouse as they swiftly walked down the street.

Later that day at the office, the coworkers were making plans, almost a daily ritual for this group. "Lisa, we're going out for drinks after work. Are you in?" Tom asked her, walking by Mags desk without even looking her way.

"Yeah, and maybe a little dancing..." Kelly chimed in, taking Tom's hand and starting to spin around.

"Alright people, remember this is an office, not a nightclub," Lisa spoke up.

"Right, this is not the club. It has better music!" Adam, the only over 30-year-old in this group of 20 somethings, laughed, "So, is that a yes, Lisa?"

"Of course, I'll be there," Lisa answered.

Tom looked at Mags, "What about you Miss Mags? Do you want to go out with the office crew tonight?"

Howard, the accounts manager, stood up and took a step toward the group. He knew how this scene was about to play out. He had witnessed it many times but he could never muster up the strength to speak out to stop it. Once again, his own shyness overtook him and he turned and sat back down disappointed in himself.

"No, thank you." Mags couldn't stand these people. They liked to party, a lot, and in her opinion the whole group was loud and obnoxious; except for Lisa, she was Mags' one and only true friend.

Kelly walked over to Mags and, looking straight at her, said, "Poor Mags can't go out and have a good time. She has to go home and feed her cat, or is it cats?" The whole group laughed; Lisa didn't think it was funny.

She looked at the group that now encircled Mags' desk; like vultures waiting for their prey, they awaited the next joke. "If Mags doesn't want to go, she doesn't want to go. Leave her alone and get back to work, everybody!" They all walked away and Mags smiled at her friend. "Besides, you don't even have a cat," Lisa said quietly and they both laughed.

When the work day was finished, Mags was the first one out the door. Lisa hurried to catch up. "Mags, are you sure you don't want to go out with us tonight? What about just you and me? We could grab dinner together, just like old times."

"No thanks," Mags shook her head.

"Mags, we've been best friends since elementary school. When we were in high school and your parents were killed in that horrible car crash, you came to live with my family. That's when we became more than friends, we became sisters. Then we went to college together, and now we work together. Why, we even live in apartments next to each other."

Mags interrupted, "I appreciate all you and your parents have done for me, you know I do. But why the trip down memory lane right now?"

"Your friendship means so much to me. I just feel like we have been growing in different directions lately," Lisa answered. "You spend too much time alone. Be careful or you might end up being the lady with all the cats and no life!"

"Lisa, it's alright. We'll get together soon. I promise. We're best friends, sisters, always. I just have to go home now." Mags hugged Lisa and said, "Just don't be mad." Then she turned and started to run away towards her apartment building.

Mags made one quick stop before she got home. She was wanting to get back to sleep so immediately that she ran into a drugstore and bought a bottle of sleeping pills. Getting home, she quickly changed clothes and read the bottle, "Take one pill for a full night's sleep. Only take if you have eight hours to devote to sleeping."

She poured a glass of water and opened the bottle of pills. "Well, if one works, then two should work faster," she reasoned to herself. Mags swallowed two sleeping pills and hurried to get into bed.

Chapter 3

"And the Winds Blow"

Magnolia was curled up by the palm tree that had sheltered her overnight. Gentle raindrops started to fall, softening her parched lips. As she opened her eyes, she felt her head throbbing. She sat up looking out at the ocean that had lulled her to sleep with its melodic sound. It was a changed scene. The once peaceful waves roared ashore. Dark clouds loomed in the distance. The winds were blowing sand strongly enough to get in her eyes.

Magnolia stood up feeling weak and dizzy. She said to herself, "I have to find something to eat and drink." Looking around, she found a coconut that had been blown down to the ground. After finding rocks to break it open, this simple coconut became a lifesaving drink and meal for the lost young lady.

She first drank the coconut water, then she devoured the meat inside the hull. By the time she had finished what she considered to be a gourmet meal the rain had gotten heavier, and the wind had really begun to pick up.

The sound of the ocean was loud and angry. The tide was coming in all the way up to the sand dunes. The rain was coming in bands. Magnolia realized this was not a simple rainstorm. A huge bolt of lightning lit up the sky that had been darkened by the clouds. Immediately afterwards, the ground shook from the thunder.

Magnolia felt strengthened by her island delicacy. She decided she should try to reach the light she had seen in the distance the night before. She hoped there was a shelter where she could go to get out of this rapidly approaching storm.

The rain was coming down now with such a blinding force that she had to shield her eyes with her hand. Looking across the dunes she could, once again, see the light. But it seemed so far away.

"It's my only chance! I must get out of this storm!" she yelled loudly, but there was no one to hear her. Soaked to the bone and trembling from the cold rain that was now no longer tiny droplets to moisten her lips but huge drops that pounded against her face and body.

Just as she thought this storm could not cause any more pain, the rain bands stopped and the winds blew in hurricane force strength. The sand pelted her body. Each grain felt as if it were a needle stabbing her as the wind blasted it against her exposed skin.

With her head bent down and her hands protecting her eyes, she trudged on. She was thankful when the next rain band came; at least the blinding rain kept the sand from stinging. Now she knew for sure that she was in the outer bands of a hurricane! How bad it would get, she couldn't know.

As she climbed the sand dune, heading toward the light, a powerful wave came in and pushed her down. As it rolled back out to sea, she stood up. She could see the light she was heading for through the sheeting rain.

One small light in a world of darkness, cold, soaking rain, painful wind, and cracking lightning strikes gave Magnolia hope that she could and would survive! A light, a beacon, a hope in this storm. Hope that there would be a shelter strong enough to protect her from the monster that was about to blow through.

The next wave came in higher and stronger than the first. It pushed Magnolia off her feet. She grabbed onto a palm tree and held on for dear life; because that's what it meant, her life! She held on until the wave had subsided.

Each wave was more violent and intense than the one before. She knew she couldn't continue much longer or go much further. Weakness, hunger, cold, and fear were overtaking her mind and body as she walked along. The blinding rain made it impossible to see where she was going. Finally, she looked up and there, right in front of her, was the structure that housed her protective light!

She could only see a few inches in front of her, but what she saw brought a sense of relief. It was a lighthouse!

There was a wooden deck surrounding it. She could see the steps just in front of her. As she started for them, she heard a loud "CRACK!" and then a "THUMP!" that was louder than even the storm. A tree had blown over and fell across the steps blocking her way into safety!

Magnolia called out, "Is anyone there? Please help me!" But no one could hear her cries for help.

The deck was ten feet above the ground with boards crossing the posts. The tide had now come all the way up to the lighthouse. One large wave knocked Magnolia to the ground. She scrambled to get up, grabbing hold of the deck post. She held on tight as the wave pounded against her.

Finally, she was able to pull herself up to the deck floor. She called out for help again, "Please, can anyone hear me?"

She reached up to the bottom rail with her right hand and grabbed on. Another wave hit her. She was losing her grip. The storm surge had reached her and was pulling her body away from the board she was clinging onto. As she tried to yell out again for help, she gagged on the ocean water.

She was holding onto that rail for dear life, literally. Barely able to breathe, choking from swallowing the salt water, her fingers were slipping off the rail. Just as her fingers slid off her last hold on life, a hand came over the top rail and grabbed her arm.

With her left hand, she grabbed hold of the arm, and immediately she was swung over the rail onto the deck. As her feet touched the floorboards, the water's great strength pushed Magnolia and her rescuer against the wall. He put his arms around her and shielded her from the impact with his body.

He quickly swept her up into his arms and carried her through the raging waters to the other side of the deck. He pushed the front door in. Magnolia was weak from her hunger and thirst. Now she was exhausted from fighting the storm. She was still coughing from gagging on the water as he gently laid her on the couch.

As she pushed her hair back from her face, Magnolia looked up to see who she could thank for saving her life. All she could see was the blanket he was shaking out to throw over her. As the blanket gently floated down over this frozen and exhausted young woman, the room went black.

Chapter 4

"The Corporate World"

Office work for Mags had always been something she "had" to do, not something she enjoyed. She was quite the opposite of Lisa, who "lived" for the corporate world.

Monitek was a new, small company on the world scene. Having received an award for being the fastest growing company in land development for the year, the boss, William, was determined to build on that accomplishment.

William was never in his office. He preferred always being out in the field working on-site inspections or meeting with people drumming up more business.

This left a very eager Lisa, his assistant, to run the office. She liked to make sure that the business ran like a well-oiled machine. On the rare occasion that the boss did come in, Lisa insisted that everything be perfect; all i's dotted and t's crossed. Everything had to be in its proper place.

Mags always called her best friend a "perfectionist." Lisa had to be in control of every aspect of her life. She didn't like or want any surprises, good or bad, at work or in her personal life. Routine and order were her comfort zone.

Mags was a different sort of girl from the start. She was a free spirit, never letting things get her down and certainly never wasting time on what she considered to be the mundane and unimportant matters in life. This girl liked to let the day happen and see where it led her, never making plans or following a schedule.

Lisa had called for an early morning meeting of the staff. The staff being herself, Mags, Howard, Kelly, Tom, and Adam. She always made it sound bigger and more important than it was.

When everyone made their way into the conference room, with coffee and donuts in hand, they all took their assigned seats; another of Lisa's ideas. But there was one seat very obviously empty, that one was assigned to Mags. Lisa looked at the chair where her best friend, adopted sister, and employee should be sitting, "Where are you, Mags?" she said under her breath.

"I'm sure Mags will be here soon. She probably just overslept," Howard spoke up to defend her. He wanted to ask the blonde haired, beauty out on a date but he had not even worked up the nerve to really talk to her. Howard always stayed at his desk in the corner of the office and watched as she greeted clients. Sometimes he would smile at her as she walked by his desk going to the copy machine. He would stop working when she answered the phone, just so he could listen to her soft voice. Unfortunately for Howard, Mags did not have the slightest idea that he was attracted to her, nor did she return his interest.

Mags had always believed that when she met the right man, the one she would give her heart to forever, she would know instantly! They would look in each other's eyes, and a connection would be made that they both would feel. This connection would involve both heart and mind. She felt they would each love and understand the other, emotionally and intellectually. Mags truly believed that when she met "him" they would immediately become linked together, forever.

Therefore, this brilliant, talented, beautiful, young woman never dated any man more than once. If that connection wasn't there, she had no need to see him again. She had never fallen in love at first sight, and that was what she was waiting for.

By lunchtime, Mags came through the office door. "Where have you been?" Lisa asked her, with arms crossed, looking more like a big sister than a boss, "You missed the staff meeting this morning."

"Oh, Lisa, you know very well that your 'staff meetings' are just a chance for you to blow your own horn about being assistant to the boss. Anyway, I overslept."

"Again! You overslept again! That's all you do these days, Mags! Sleep!" Lisa was more than a little annoyed.

"Lisa, I had that dream again. It was so real! I just can't wake up when I'm dreaming. I feel like—"

Lisa interrupted her friend, "Mags, I'm starting to worry about you. This is getting serious. You seem to be more involved in your 'dream world' than in 'reality.'" Lisa was no longer annoyed, now she was just concerned.

Howard chose this moment to intervene. He walked by the two young women with his lunch bag in his hand. Every day it was the same lunch, a sandwich, pickle, chips, and a cookie in a brown paper bag. He drank from a recycled cup he refilled with water from the office cooler.

"Have you had lunch yet, Mags?" he asked, holding up his brown paper bag, as if to offer to share his lunch with her.

"Thanks. I'm good," Mags said, never even looking at Howard, just taking the opportunity to walk away from Lisa.

Kelly, the original party girl, seemed to derive great pleasure from torturing Mags over her simple lifestyle. "Did your cat forget to wake you up this morning, Mags?"

she asked as she sauntered by the receptionist's desk on her way out to lunch. Tom and Adam laughed as they caught up to her. "Lisa, are you coming to lunch with us?" Kelly asked.

"Sure," Lisa answered, "Try and hold down the fort till we get back, Mags. Do you want me to bring you something?"

"No thanks, I'm fine." She was just happy they were leaving the office.

"Alone at last," Mags said to herself, forgetting Howard was still at his desk. She took a leather-backed journal out of her bag and picked up her pen. She began to write, "I don't know how to explain what has been happening to me. It's as though my concept of reality has somehow been altered. My feelings in my dreams are more real to me than what I feel in this, what they call 'reality.' I feel empty in this 'reality,' but in my 'dream world,' I feel alive and whole, completely fulfilled as a person."

Howard saw Mags sitting quietly at her desk, looking as if she were a million miles away. He opened the drawer and took out a flower he had picked on his way to work that morning. He got up slowly from his chair so as not to startle the one he secretly held a torch for... or maybe not so secretly.

Just as he walked up behind her, the office door opened and in walked the rest of the Monitek crew. Howard looked up at the group and froze, standing there with a flower in his hand.

Tom saw the surprise and embarrassment on Howard's face. "Well, look at that! Our little Howard was about to make a move on Mags."

Adam broke in with, "Look out Mags, you might not be able to resist those paper bag lunches he will offer you."

Kelly took the opportunity to add her input, laughing as she walked by Howard, who was still frozen in place behind Mags' chair. As she was reapplying her lipstick, she said, "Hey, Mags, maybe a little make-up would help. Oh, wait!" she laughed again, "You two are perfect for each other just as you are...the nerd and the cat lady!"

Mags spun her chair around to see what all her coworkers were laughing about. She saw Howard, standing there behind her, with a flower in his hand, ready to give it to her. When she looked at him, he turned and walked back to his desk, crumpling the flower on the way.

Lisa walked into the office and, not knowing what was going on, said, "Lunch is over people. Let's get back to work."

Chapter 5

"Back to the Beach"

It was pitch black inside the room where Magnolia found herself. She could hear glass rattle. When she looked in the direction of the sound she saw someone coming toward her carrying a lantern. She could hear the waves pounding against the walls outside and the howling of the winds as they blew a shiver down her spine.

He brought the lantern closer to her and she could see in the pale light the silhouette of her rescuer. All she knew was that he was muscular in build and soaking wet too. And she was very, very grateful for him saving her! He set the lantern down and walked away. Magnolia was still shivering from the cold rain she had spent hours walking through. She sat up and tried to reach for the lantern. Feeling weak and dizzy, she laid back against the couch.

He came back into the light with folded clothes in his hand. "Here," he reached his hand out to her, "let me help you." She took his hand and stood up. He wrapped the blanket around her. Holding tightly onto her, he walked her to the next room where a lantern was already lit. "You go in here and get that wet dress off. These are mine, but they will have to do for now."

She smiled as she caught a glimpse of his face in the flickering light. As she pulled away from his arm, he saw her for the first time. His heart jumped as she turned back toward him and simply and quietly said, "Thank you." He pulled the door shut and stood there thinking to himself, "Is it? Could it be? Her?" He went to the kitchen while still looking back toward the bedroom door.

Magnolia walked over to the bed, took the blanket from around her and laid it across the foot of the bed. She shivered as she dropped her sundress to the floor. She picked up the t-shirt she had been given to wear. She smelled it as she slowly pulled it over her head. "This is a moment I am going to remember forever," she thought to herself. It smelled of fresh salt air, reminding her of when she first opened her eyes on the beach and how peaceful and calm everything was.

Next, she stepped into the jeans. They were big on her, but she felt so comfortable in them. Everything about this place made her feel relaxed and at home but most of all safe. She picked her dress up from the floor and walked over to another door. She hung it on the doorknob to dry. She looked at the dresser where the lantern was. It was an antique, rather worn, matching the 4-poster bed that took up most of the room.

Magnolia ran her fingers across the dresser as she walked back to the door she had come in. Just as her hand touched the doorknob, there was a soft knock at the door. "Are you alright in there?" The concern in his voice made her smile.

She leaned against the door and took a deep breath, "Yes, I'm just coming out," she answered as she opened the door.

"I started a fire to warm you, and I had a pot of hot soup on the stove before I lost power." He motioned toward the warm and inviting fireplace.

Magnolia walked over to the fire and sat down in front of it, warming her hands. She turned toward him, but he was gone. After a few minutes, he reappeared with a bowl of piping hot soup for her. "Here, you eat this while I go batten down a few more hatches. This storm is a lot worse than I expected."

She sat by the fire, warming herself, eating the soup, and she said to herself, "I am so thankful to be here... wherever here is."

A few minutes later, the front door slammed as a very wet young man came through it. She watched him as he shook the water from his blonde hair.

He left his shoes by the door and, as he went into the bedroom, he said, "I guess it's my turn on put on some dry clothes." Soon he came back out, all dried off and walked over to the fireplace. "Would you like some more soup?" he asked her.

"No thank you. But it was very good," Magnolia said.

He sat down by her and took her bowl and set it on the hearth. "By the way, I'm Jess."

She smiled, "Hi Jess. I'm Magnolia. Thank you for saving me."

Picking up the fire poker, Jess looked at her, "You're safe now. This lighthouse has stood on this island for over a hundred years. She has seen many storms." He stoked the fire to warm them up more.

"So...we're on an island?" Magnolia questioned him.

"Well, yes. Don't you know where you are? How did you get here? I thought you must have been trying to outrun the hurricane and left your boat at the dock," Jess replied.

"No. I don't know where I am or how I got here. All I know is that yesterday I was on a beautiful, peaceful beach. Today, I was being swept away by the storm surge, and then you saved me."

"Where did you come from? Weren't you on a boat?" Jess asked her as he put another log on the fire.

"I just don't know. I don't remember anything. All I know is that my name is Magnolia and I am safe...and hungry! Could I have some more of that delicious soup please?" They both laughed as Jess picked up her bowl and went into the kitchen.

The wind howled outside the concrete based lighthouse. Magnolia couldn't see the lightening flashing because Jess had closed the shutters on the windows but she could still hear the thunder.

Just as Jess came back with her soup, another bolt of lightning struck right outside of the lighthouse. The thunder cracked so loud that it caused a shiver to go down Magnolia's still cold and shaking spine.

Jess handed her the bowl of hot soup and picked up a throw from a chair to wrap around her. "I guess it's going to take a while to get you warm." He sat down on the floor behind her and rubbed her arms trying to get her blood flowing. She sat quietly, staring into the flickering flames, almost losing herself in thought.

"Can this be real? It feels so 'right.' I feel like I belong here; like I've always belonged here," she thought to herself. She put the bowl down and turned to look at Jess.

Another loud crack from the storm outside made her jump. He put his arms around her and held her tightly.

Without a word being said their eyes met. He whispered quietly, "It is you."

She eventually stopped shivering as they peacefully sat together looking at the fire, smelling the wood burning and listening to the storm raging on the other side of the walls. It could have lasted a few minutes or several hours; neither of them knew. Time seemed to have stopped on this island for these young people.

In the warmth of the fire, the safety of the lighthouse and the strength of the arms still around her, Magnolia finally spoke, "I don't hear anything. It's quiet outside."

Jess stood up. "Yes, I think it's finally over." He reached out his hand to help Magnolia up.

"What now?" she asked.

"Now..." he took a deep breath and exhaled, "I assess the damage and start cleaning up and repairing. The weather forecasters called for a category 4 storm. I think it was stronger than that. I'm just thankful for the speed that it blew through. It was a strong but very fast moving storm."

He walked to the front door and opened it. Warm, bright sunlight streamed through into the living room. He stepped out onto the deck, at least onto what remained of it. Turning back toward Magnolia, he said, "You better stay inside until I see if it's safe to move around out here."

She stood inside watching from the doorway as he threw branches off the deck. He opened the shutters on the windows and clean, fresh air filled the living quarters of the lighthouse. As the sunlight brightened the dark room, Magnolia could clearly see all the surroundings. As she looked around she saw paintings, beautiful, familiar paintings. There were paintings of the beach, where she had found herself lying in the sand. On another wall, there hung paintings of the sand dunes she had climbed. And finally, she saw a painting of a lighthouse, with the light glowing in the darkness that engulfed it. "My saving light," she said to herself.

"You can come out. Just watch where you step. Boards are missing from the deck and the downed tree has the steps blocked. But we can get around," he said as he reached for her hand.

They walked together to the other side of the deck. From that vantage point they could see the beach. The calmness of the ocean showed no signs of the monster that had just ransacked Jess' island home.

"It's so peaceful again," Magnolia said as she gazed out over the horizon.

"The ocean is peaceful but look around you." Jess pointed to fallen trees and debris strewn up and down the beach. In the distance, she could see a boat dock.

Jess immediately started the cleanup. "The first thing I have to do is get this tree off the steps so we can get around." He jumped over the rail of the deck and landed on his feet. He made his way through the debris to another dwelling that remained intact.

Magnolia watched Jess going into what looked like a small house a short distance away. Soon he was back with a chain saw and started cutting up the tree that had blocked Magnolia's steps to safety from the storm.

As Jess finished cutting the tree into moveable sized pieces, Magnolia came down the steps. When Jess picked up one end of the log she grabbed the other end to help him carry it to the woodpile; at least to what remained of it. The storm had spread most of the firewood around the island.

"Is that your neighbor's house?" she asked, pointing to the small dwelling where he had gotten the chain saw.

"No. This lighthouse has been here for over one hundred years. In the beginning, all the lightkeepers were men alone. But sometime later, one of the keepers brought his family here to live with him. The lighthouse's living quarters were too small for a growing family, so he built that small cottage for his family and him to live in."

"So...where are your neighbors?" Magnolia asked with a questioning look on her face.

"Magnolia," he said as they lifted another log, "I have no neighbors. I live on this island completely alone. That's how I've wanted it...until now."

"But how do you get by? I mean...all by yourself?" she asked him.

Once the steps were cleared, Jess said, "Come on, I'll show you."

He took her to a small area on top of a sand dune where he had his power grid set up. "It's all solar power here, everything from the lighthouse to the keeper's cottage. It all runs on solar power, dependent only on the sun, which we get plenty of here. The power is out at the lighthouse because the storm broke a connection somewhere. I just have to find it and fix it. Then we will be up and running again."

Magnolia sat down on the sand and watched Jess work. As he made the needed repairs, he would occasionally look her way. She tried not to, but it made her smile, which, in turn, made him smile.

She was still wearing his pants and t-shirt. Now that the sun was out, it was getting hot. Magnolia rolled the pant legs up and laid back in the sand, feeling the warm sun on her face. It was such a contrast from the cold she had experienced just a few hours earlier that she drifted off to sleep.

Chapter 6

"The Journal"

After a very long and, to Mags, an extremely boring day at work, it was finally quitting time. "How about grabbing a bite to eat before we head home?" Lisa asked Mags as she was packing her overloaded bag to head home. "Come on, you promised me days ago, that we could get together. How about it?"

The last thing Mags stuffed into her bag was the one thing she couldn't live without, her most valuable possession, her journal. She took it everywhere that she went. She wrote in it constantly. It held her thoughts, her feelings, her hopes, and her dreams. Especially lately. Her "dream world" had overwhelmed her "reality." And she didn't want to forget a detail. She wrote everything down. It was only for her to read. She never even let her best friend, Lisa, have a glance.

"Sure Lisa. Let's go," she said as they walked away from her desk.

As she slung her bag over her shoulder her journal fell out.

Howard was on his way out and saw it hit the floor. "Hey, Mags." He tried to stop her but she and Lisa were chatting and already out of the door. He reached to pick it up to leave it in her desk but saw it had fallen open to a page that caught his eye. He picked up the journal and looked around. He was the last person in the office. He sat down at Mags' desk.

The page where the journal had opened was her last entry. Howard couldn't believe what he was reading and he couldn't stop himself.

"I've met someone. Someone who makes me feel whole, complete. He fills a need in me. A need that's as basic to life as breathing air. I feel as if I've been drowning in the ocean and I've just come up from the water and taken a deep breath of air. As if my lungs are filled and my body is floating on top of the waves with the warm sunlight shining on my face."

Howard stopped reading and sat there in Mags' chair. "Could it be that she has finally realized that I am the only one for her? Has she sensed my love for her and fallen secretly in love with me? I know I should put her journal up but I have to read more." He continued reading.

"It is him. He is the very air that I take into my lungs for survival. When I first saw his face, it was that lifesaving gasp of oxygen as I came up from drowning in this sea of life. But how do I let him know that I completely adore him? Should I tell him? How does he feel about me?

Suppose he doesn't return my love. No! I can't even imagine life without him. He loves me. He has to."

Howard closed the book. "Yes, Mags, I do. And I will show you." He put her journal in her desk drawer and got up from the chair. "It must have been when I tried to give her the flower. That's when she realized her feelings for me." Howard walked to the office door, looked back at Mags' desk imagining her sitting there, turned out the lights and left, locking the door behind him.

Howard spent the evening very excitedly researching flowers. A stray flower picked up on the way to work just wouldn't do now. He wanted to give his secret love something special, a symbol of what their love means to him, and now, he's sure, to her. It had to show his devotion, a flower that would continue to bloom as their love blossomed and grow as their relationship deepened.

Lisa and Mags were sitting at their regular table in their favorite restaurant, waiting for their food. Lisa was sipping on wine and chatting about her latest accomplishment at work when she realized that Mags was staring off into space. "Mags! Where are you?" she snapped at her friend.

"I'm sitting right here in front of you, Lisa. Listening to you drone on about work. Lisa!" She got very excited all of a sudden. "I have something to tell you! It's important to me that you try to understand."

Lisa put down her glass of wine. "Of course, I'll understand. Don't I always?"

Mags continued, "I've met someone. Oh, Lisa! He's wonderful! He's kind and warm and thoughtful. He's a good, hard worker too. And good looking… Oh so handsome with his blonde hair and blue eyes."

"Where? When? How? When do I get to meet him?" Now, Lisa was excited for her friend and interrupted the description of her dream man.

"Well…" Mags paused, not knowing how to say the next words. Then, they just sort of flowed out. "I have only seen him in my dreams. But I know he is real! Lisa, I just know it!"

"Mags! No! Not that again! You cannot live in that 'dream world' of yours. You have to live in 'reality', my 'reality, our 'reality'!" People were starting to look at the two young women as their voices were getting louder with their emotional outbursts.

"You said you would try to understand. Why won't you even give me a chance to explain?" Mags begged.

"What is there to explain? That you would rather sleep and dream than live your real life?" Lisa lowered her voice as she saw the people staring. "Be careful who you tell this fantasy to, Mags. They are liable to lock you away."

The waiter brought the food and interrupted the, now quiet, argument between Lisa and Mags. And neither one of them brought the subject up again that night.

Howard's research brought him to, what he considered to be, the perfect flower to give to his secret love. He said aloud, "The sunflower symbolizes adoration, loyalty and longevity. This is perfect! I absolutely adore her. No matter what comes, I will always be loyal to my love. And I know our love will last for as long as we live." Howard closed his laptop. "But I won't give her just a flower. I'll give her a small potted sunflower so it can grow as our love grows and it can live on endlessly."

Chapter 7

"Cleaning Up"

"Hey sleepy head! I'm all finished here. We should have power back at the lighthouse. Are you ready to wake up?" Jess asked her reaching out his hand to help her up.

Magnolia woke up, a little confused at first about where she was. But then she looked up and saw Jess. She reached out and took his hand. As they walked together back to the lighthouse, Magnolia thought to herself, "I could get used to this."

Once they were back at the lighthouse, Magnolia went in the bedroom to put her sundress on. She could hear voices coming from the living room but couldn't tell who Jess was talking to or what they were saying.

Then he knocked on the bedroom door. "I have the two-way radio back up and working. I talked to the tower. I asked my friend, Joe, to check for any missing persons reports. If there is one out on you, we can find out how Magnolia-without-a-memory got to the island. Now I have to go up the beach and check on the dock and boat. Do you want to come?"

Before he could finish asking the question, Magnolia came running out of the bedroom. "Yes!" she shouted.

"Well, I don't know whether to take that as you want to go with me or you want to check on the boat so you can get away from me." They both laughed.

As they walked up the beach they found pieces of wood, fiberglass, and life rings. "It looks as though someone's boat broke up in that storm," Jess said as he picked up a life vest. He looked at Magnolia. She was staring out over the ocean with a very solemn look on her face.

"Come on," he said, trying to lighten the mood, "let's check on the dock."

When they got to the dock everything was a mess, including the boat. It was battered and beaten but still afloat. "I hope you weren't wanting to get away from me anytime soon." He picked up a broken board and tossed it over to what seemed like a pile of rubbish. "This is going to take a while to fix."

"That's alright with me," she said, again looking very solemn. "I don't even know where I would go."

As Jess was checking on the pylons that once held the dock up, Magnolia wandered over to the pile where he had thrown the board. There was a bright orange object that caught her eye. She started pulling boards and seaweed away from it to see what it was.

Suddenly she screamed, "Jess! Jess! Come help me!"

He ran to her in an instant, "What is it?"

"I found something, a box maybe. I can't get to it," she said.

He pulled the rest of the trash off and lifted the box out of the pile and set it on the beach. "It's a dry box. We use them on boats to keep things… well… dry. It's waterproof. At least it should be. Let's find out."

He started to unlatch the top of the plastic box when Magnolia grabbed his hand. "Wait! I have a bad feeling about this."

"What are you thinking? The boat debris, the life vest, now this box. You keep looking out over the ocean longingly. Were you in the boat when it broke up?" Jess asked her.

They both sat down in the sand together. Magnolia looked toward him. She had tears streaming down her face. "I don't know, Jess. I just don't know. I found myself on this beach with no memory except my name. Suppose it was my boat? And if it is my box, what do I find in it? Will it tell me who I am? Where I came from? How I got here? Maybe I don't want to know."

"That's completely understandable. You have been through a lot in the last couple of days. Somehow you were stranded on this island. And then you managed to survive a hurricane with the storm surge trying to sweep you away." He reached over and wiped the tears from her face. "I will tell you what. Why don't I put this box in a safe place, so it won't get washed back out to the sea. Then, when and if you want to open it, we will."

"Yes, thank you, Jess," Magnolia said.

"For now, let's go back to the lighthouse and have some supper. It's getting late and all this storm recovery has made me hungry," Jess said.

As they walked along the beach, the sun was setting behind the dunes. The sky was about to put on its nightly show of the color spectrum. Jess and Magnolia stopped occasionally to watch the pelicans diving for their supper. Magnolia laughed as she saw the Sand Pipers running along in front of them.

As they topped the sand dune, the sun was just about to drop into the horizon. They stood in awe of the spectacular color extravaganza they were witnessing.

"This is the most beautiful sunset I have ever seen," Jess said quietly. Then he turned to Magnolia and said, "While you are here, the lighthouse is yours. I'll be staying in the lightkeeper's house." Magnolia smiled at him. She felt at home, safe and welcome.

After watching the sun drop into the horizon, the two walked back to the lighthouse and went inside. "There is still some soup left, if you want to warm it up," Jess said as he went into the bedroom.

Magnolia got the soup ready and Jess came out with his backpack. Magnolia put the bowls of soup on the table in the cozy dining area next to the kitchen. She looked over at the fireplace, where she had felt so warm and comfortable earlier. "The fire has gone out," she said.

"We don't have much need of the fireplace until the weather gets colder or a storm blows through," Jess said as he put his backpack on the couch and sat down to eat.

"Sad. I really enjoyed the fire. It was so peaceful," Magnolia said as she sat down with him.

"I laid out a few more clothes for you, some t-shirts and shorts. Oh, and a belt to hold them up." They both laughed. "You'll find a new toothbrush in the bathroom. I want you to feel at home here."

"Thank you," Magnolia said as they started clearing away the finished supper dishes. "I already do."

After cleaning up from supper together, Jess picked up his backpack. "Just one thing," he said as he walked over to a door on the other side of the room, "don't go in here. It's not safe."

"Does that door lead to the stairs that go up to the light?" Magnolia asked.

"Yes, it does. Please promise me that you won't go in there. It's too dangerous," Jess said.

"I promise," she said. "I think I've had enough adventure lately."

Jess smiled. He walked out the front door leaving Magnolia alone for the night.

Chapter 8

"I'm Here"

Howard left for work early to stop by the local plant nursery to buy a special gift for that special someone.

"Can I help you?" the lady watering the flowers asked him.

"No thank you. I have to find the best one. It has to be perfect," he said back to her. "Perfect...just like she is," he said under his breath. After meticulously going through every sunflower in the greenhouse, he finally chose the one. After paying for it, he hurried to get to the office before anyone else. As he sat it down on Mags' desk, he picked up the card that came with it. He wrote something on it and put it in the envelope, then he carefully placed it on the flower.

No one noticed Howard sitting quietly at his desk as they filed in for the work day. But then, they never did. It was the usual morning chatter, who did what the night before and what each of them had for breakfast.

It was Kelly that noticed the flower on Mags' desk, just as Mags and Lisa came through the door. "Oh! Look! Mags has an admirer."

"What are you talking about, Kelly?" Lisa asked as she walked across the office.

Mags saw the flower and sat down at her desk trying to act like nothing was going on.

"Who is it from, Mags? Don't leave us in suspense?" Kelly goaded her on.

"Where did this come from? Did anyone see who put this here?" Lisa asked looking around the room. No one answered her. Howard tried to look busy while keeping an eye on the situation.

Mags took a deep breath and sighed, wondering if this was a trick set up by the office crew. She imagined they were waiting for her disappointment when she found out that it was a joke. They would have a good laugh at her expense, she thought.

"There is a card," Lisa said.

Mags picked up the envelope. Howard was watching from his desk. His heart was pounding so loudly he was afraid everyone could hear it. He thought it would burst out of his chest at any second. His palms were sweating. "Will she look at me after she reads the card? Or will she want to keep our feelings secret...for now?" He had a million thoughts and questions running through his mind.

Mags opened the envelope. She read it silently. Just two words, "I'm here," was all it said. She could hardly believe her eyes! Two simple words but they meant more to Mags than she could ever express. More than she could possibly have imagined or hoped for!

"I'm here." "Is it true? Is he here?" The thoughts running through her mind were almost too much for her to handle. How could she contain her excitement, her feelings? "I'm here." "Could it be my Jess?" she thought, she hoped.

Her private thoughts were interrupted by an almost unanimous, "Well?" coming from the crowd that had gathered around her desk.

"It's...nobody. Just a mistake from the florist." Mags tried to conceal her overwhelming emotions.

"I knew it was too good to be true. Who would be sending her flowers anyway?" Kelly acted as if she was almost disappointed as they all went to their desks to start the work day.

All except Lisa. She kept standing by Mags until everyone was gone. "Really Mags, who is it from?"

"I told you, nobody," Mags said as she got to work.

"Fine, if that's how you want it. Just remember, I'm here, if you want to talk," Lisa said as she walked away.

"I'm here." Mags kept running those two words over and over in her mind. She slowly looked around the office to see if anyone was watching her. As her eyes met

Howard's, he slightly smiled. She continued to scan the office, not even acknowledging him at all.

When she was sure nobody was watching her, except maybe Howard, but he didn't matter, she opened her bag to put away the card. "Oh no! My journal! My journal is gone!" she screamed.

Lisa ran over, "What's wrong? Did something happen?"

"Lisa, I can't find my journal. It's gone! You know I always keep it in my bag. You know that! It's not here!" she said as she was dumping her bag out on her desk.

"Calm down," Lisa urged her. "It's got to be around here somewhere."

Howard got up from his desk, thinking he might have to say something about finding it the night before. He hoped he wouldn't have to. He was afraid that if she knew he had read any part of her private journal, it could ruin their relationship before it even got started.

"Check your desk. Maybe it's in one of the drawers," Lisa said as she pulled open the top drawer.

"I never put it in a drawer. Suppose someone found it and read it. That journal contains my most intimate thoughts and feelings. I would never leave it..." Mags looked down at the opened drawer and there was her journal! "How did it get there?" she asked herself quietly.

Howard breathed a sigh of relief and went back to his desk in the back of the office. He was thankful no one had noticed him.

"I'm telling you, Mags," Lisa said in a very concerned tone of voice, "you have got to get control of yourself. All these dreams and now you're losing things. You need to get a grip on 'reality' before something bad happens."

Mags just sat there, quietly, as Lisa walked away, shaking her head. Then Mags opened the journal and put the card inside it. She closed it and put it in the bottom of her bag. For the next few minutes she did nothing but sit in that spot and look at that sunflower. She thought of her Jess and those two words, "I'm here."

At lunchtime, Lisa came to Mags' desk, "You know I'm really sorry about our argument last night. We're best friends, sisters. I just want what is best for you."

"I know Lisa. I'm sorry, too," Mags said.

"How about lunch today, with me and the office crew?" Lisa asked.

"I don't know, Lisa. You know how I feel about them."

"Mags, you will never meet anyone just sitting in this office and staying home at night!" Lisa was getting annoyed.

Mags thought to herself, "She is right. If I'm going to find Jess, I have to get out there." Mags grabbed her bag and stood up. "You're right, Lisa, let's go."

Howard overheard the conversation and ran ahead of them to open the door. "Do you mind if I join the crew for lunch?" Howard asked.

Lisa answered Howard, "Of course! You and Mags are part of the office crew."

When all three of them walked into the restaurant, Kelly saw them. "It must be 'take a geek to lunch day,'" she said to Tom, and they both laughed.

Adam waved his hand in the air, "We're over here!" They pulled up an extra table and chairs to fit the rest of the group. "So, what brings our little Mags out of the office into the real world today?" Kelly sniped.

Lisa jumped in, "We thought it was time Mags got out into the world. To meet more people and live a little."

"And what about you, Mr. Paper Bag Lunch Guy?" Kelly continued. "How do we get the honor of your presence at our humble table?"

"Kelly, how about you can it for once. Let's just have a quiet, peaceful lunch," Adam spoke up.

"Well, I was just having a little fun. Trying to lighten the mood," Kelly replied.

"The mood is just fine," Lisa said as the waiter came to get their orders.

After Kelly's scolding, it was a typical lunch. Adam and Tom talked about sports scores. Lisa and Kelly discussed what they were each wearing to the club that night. Howard didn't say much, but every chance he got he looked toward Mags. Mags just ate her lunch and ignored everyone else.

As soon as he was finished eating, Howard jumped up and said, "I have to get back to the office. Those accounts don't add themselves."

"When did he become Mr. Overachiever?" Kelly asked.

When the waiter brought the tickets, he said to Mags, "Your bill has already been paid."

"By who?" Lisa asked. "Who paid for her?" This big sister was getting worried.

"I don't know. It was paid for on the kiosk and the receipt was left behind." The waiter said, "Here's your receipt."

"First the flowers and now this? Maybe our little girl does have a secret admirer," Kelly said.

Mags picked up the receipt to put it in her bag, and she noticed something written on the back. She held it on her lap so no one could see her reading it. "I'm here," those same two words written on the receipt were now beginning to torture her. "Where?" she accidently said out loud.

"The club, silly. We said we are going to the club after work," Kelly responded thinking Mags was listening to their conversation.

"Are you alright?" Lisa asked Mags. "You know, it is alright to have a secret admirer. It could be kind of fun. Why don't you go with us to the club tonight and see if he follows you? Who knows, maybe you will even find out who he is."

"Yeah, why don't you join us? You might enjoy yourself. Even Howard comes out with us sometimes," Adam encouraged her.

They left the conversation open as they all got up to head back to work. Mags kept looking around her, watching for Jess to show up.

Chapter 9

"The Box"

Every morning, Magnolia found Jess up early working on the dock and his boat. And, every morning, Jess saw Magnolia standing and staring at the box she had found in the hurricane debris.

"There's only one way to stop that box from eating away at your brain. You know what you need to do. Open it," Jess said as he walked over to her. "I'll be with you. There is nothing to fear."

"I know you are right," Magnolia said as she handed Jess his morning cup of coffee.

"I don't know how I have survived so long," Jess said smiling at her, "without you here to make my coffee for me."

Magnolia smiled back at him. "You're right. I'm being silly. Fearing a box. What could it possibly hold that could hurt me." She walked over to the box and kneeled down beside it. "Will you do it for me, Jess? Will you open it?"

"Of course I will," he said as he put his coffee cup down.

He walked over to her and sat down in the sand beside her. First, he unlatched the clips. Then, he looked at her and said, "No matter what is in here, everything is going to be alright. I'm right here with you."

"I know," she said with the same look of trepidation a person would have when a dentist was about to pull their tooth, "go on and open it." She took a deep breath and said, "I'm ready."

Jess opened the top to the bright orange dry box. Magnolia leaned over it slowly, as if she thought something were about to jump out and bite her. But nothing happened. To her surprise, everything seemed safe and normal and, apparently, hers. As she started to take things out, she was very happy that they had finally opened the box.

"Well, I guess we know for sure who was on that boat when it broke up. Unless there is another young lady stranded on an island somewhere that likes to wear cute little sundresses," Jess said as he held up one sundress after another.

"Point made," Magnolia laughed as she took the dresses away from him. "Oh good! A pair of flip flops. I sure am tired of running around on this hot sand barefoot."

"Do any of these things look familiar to you? Do they bring back any memories at all?" Jess asked her.

Magnolia looked at the dresses and the flip flops, "No, they don't." Then she smiled and said, "But I sure do have good taste!" They were both laughing when Magnolia pulled the last item out of the dry box. It was wrapped alone in a dry bag.

"It's a journal!" Jess said. "Maybe now you can find out where you are from. And where you were going."

Magnolia sat back with a worried look on her face, again. She set the journal on top of the sundresses as she slipped the flip flops on her feet.

"Aren't you going to open it?" Jess asked her.

"No, not yet. I'm not ready for that. I just want to be Magnolia-without-a-memory for a while longer."

"That's just fine with me. We know who you are as a person. Not having a memory doesn't change that. Besides, I kind of like Magnolia-without-a-memory," Jess said as he stood up. "Now I have to get back to work on the dock and boat, or we're going to be Jess and Magnolia with no supplies."

She stood up and picked up all her things. "Jess and Magnolia... I like that," she said to herself. "What happens when all the repairs are finished?" she asked.

"We go to the mainland and buy groceries and whatever other supplies we need. I usually go about once a month. Are you getting antsy to get off the island?" he asked her.

"Me? No way! I love it here! I could stay here FOREVER! I'm taking my new clothes to the lighthouse. I'll be back to help you with the repairs in a few minutes." Magnolia practically skipped away, she was so excited to have a change of clothes and to know what was in the box.

"I hope so, Magnolia," Jess said to himself as she walked away. "I hope you will stay here with me... forever."

When Magnolia went in the lighthouse, she laid all her dresses out on the bed. She chose, what she thought was, the prettiest one to put on before she went back to the beach to help Jess work. As she pulled the dress off the bed, the book she had found in the dry box fell to the floor. Magnolia picked it up and sat down on the bed. She took it out of the dry bag that it had been put in, obviously, for extra protection.

"What secrets do you hold? Do I even want to know? Will finding out where I came from take me away from where I am?" She questioned the journal as if it was a living, breathing, entity, that could answer her. "But not now. I'm happy with where I am and who I am. I don't want anything to change." She put the journal on top of the dresser.

Then, she took off the sundress that she had worn, rinsed out at night, and put back on the next morning nearly every day since she had gotten to the island. That was the routine, except for the days when she was wearing Jess' oversized shirts and jeans. She was so happy. She slipped the new sundress on and took off running back to Jess.

As she was handing Jess boards to repair the dock, Magnolia asked him, "So, what happens if we don't get the dock fixed before we run out of supplies?"

"It's not just the dock that has to be repaired." Jess pointed over at his boat. "She took a lot of damage from the storm. We can't go offshore until I know for sure that she is seaworthy."

"If we run out of supplies, do we just live off the land? You know, eating coconuts and fish?" She laughed but was a little bit curious.

"It would take quite a while for us to run completely out of food. I have a huge freezer that, thankfully, wasn't out of power long enough for the food to defrost. I also have a whole room full of dry goods and canned food in the keeper's house. I stay pretty well stocked up. But to answer your question, if we ran out of anything we really needed, I would have it flown in." He reached for her to hand him another board but she was just looking at him.

"Flown in? From where?" she asked, realizing she was falling off the job so she picked up a board.

"I could radio the tower and have whatever we need either flown in by seaplane or dropped by an airlift. But I don't like to do that," he said.

"Why not?" she asked while still standing there holding onto the board.

"Because it breaks the eggs when they hit the beach," he replied.

Magnolia realized that he was joking and started laughing.

"Of course, if you don't want to live off scrambled eggs, you need to hand me that board," Jess said.

"Oh, sorry," Magnolia said as she got back to work. "Let's get this thing finished. I don't want to live on scrambled eggs!" They both laughed.

Chapter 10

"The Dance"

The entire office crew went to the club that night. They were all sitting around a table chatting when the waitress came up to take their drink orders. "I'll have a cup of tea," Mags said. Everyone looked at her, but no one said anything.

"So will I," Howard spoke up.

"Where are we? England?" Kelly laughed.

"Leave them alone. At least Mags came out of her apartment tonight," Lisa said.

After the drinks were brought and consumed, and more were ordered, Tom and Kelly walked up on stage.

"What are they doing?" Mags asked. Lisa didn't hear her, so Howard took the opportunity to move over to the seat beside her.

"This is the part of the night where Tom and Kelly set out to see who can embarrass themselves the most. It's time for Karaoke," Howard told her.

Mags looked at Howard and laughed. "That would be a change, wouldn't it?"

That was the first time Mags ever acknowledged Howard's existence. And it was enough to make him feel positive that she returned his feelings.

"Care to dance?" Adam asked Lisa.

"As always," Lisa replied as they headed for the dancefloor.

"They all do this every night?" Mags asked Howard.

"Pretty much. I come occasionally. I always just watch and drink my tea."

When Tom and Kelly's song was over, the duo, along with Adam and Lisa, sat back down at the table. The evening continued with drinking, talking, singing, and dancing. Mags kept looking around, but she never saw anyone watching her. No one ever made eye contact with her. Finally, she sighed, "He's just not here."

"What was that, Mags?" Lisa asked her.

"I'm ready to get out of here," Mags answered Lisa. "Are you ready to go home yet?"

"Do you remember why we took a cab here, Mags?" Lisa asked her.

"Yes. Because you said we would be having so much fun that we would want to stay late and you don't drink and drive." Mags shook her head and said, "Then I'll get my own cab. See you tomorrow." Mags laid a five-dollar bill on the table to cover her cup of tea and walked to the door.

"I'm out, too," Howard said as he threw his money on the table and ran after Mags.

"Was it something we said?" Kelly laughed. Then she and Tom got up to sing another song.

"Mags! Wait!" Howard called out to her as she walked out to the street.

"I'm leaving, Howard, don't try to stop me," Mags said, thinking Lisa had sent him after her.

"No, I'm not trying to stop you. I'm leaving too. I have my car. Would you like a ride home?" Howard asked her.

"Well, if it's on your way and not too much trouble," Mags said.

"It is… I mean… it's no trouble at all," Howard walked to his car and Mags followed him.

"Electric huh?" Mags said as he opened the door for her. "You really do want to save the planet, don't you?"

"Future generations will thank us," Howard said as he closed the door after her.

The two were quiet on the drive to Mags' apartment. As he pulled up in front, Howard started to get out. "I can let myself out," Mags said.

Howard looked at her and said, "But why should you, I'm here."

As Mags turned toward him, Howard stepped out of the car. He walked around it and opened her door. She was sitting there, stunned. "Why did you say that?" she asked.

"Why did I say what? I believe chivalry is not dead. A man should open the door for a woman and carry her groceries and bring her flowers." Howard was hoping he hadn't said too much.

Mags got out of the car, still looking at Howard very strangely. "Thanks for the ride," she said as she started to walk to her apartment building.

Howard was walking behind her. As she got to the door, he held his hand out for the key. She, very hesitatingly, gave it to him. Howard unlocked the door, pushed it open, handed Mags the key back, and said, "I'll see you in the morning."

Mags stepped inside the Brownstone and slowly turned around. Howard was already in his car about to drive away.

"It can't be… Howard?" Mags said to herself. Then she ran upstairs and went into her apartment. "No! It's not Howard. It's my Jess. He is out there somewhere and I will find him," Mags said to herself, as she got ready for bed.

She tossed and turned. Finally, she got up and took a sleeping pill. But, she still couldn't fall asleep. "I'm here." Those two words were all she could think of. She got up and took another pill. "This will take me to my Jess," she said, as she went back to bed.

The next morning, Lisa was banging on Mags' door again when it was time to leave for work. "I'm coming!" Mags yelled from the bedroom. She ran out the door, still getting dressed as usual. "I'm ready," she said to Lisa.

"You look awful!" Lisa told her. "What is wrong with you?"

"I couldn't sleep last night. And when I did sleep, Lisa, I didn't dream. Lisa, my Jess wasn't there. I couldn't dream of him!" Mags sounded desperate.

"I think that's a good thing. Maybe getting out really helped you to come back to 'reality'." Lisa said as they hurried to work.

Mags tried to focus on work, but her mind kept returning to those two words, "I'm here." "But where? Where are you, Jess?" Mags thought to herself.

At lunch time, Howard walked over to Mags' desk. "Do you have plans for lunch?" he asked.

"No, I'm going to just work through lunch today," Mags said to him.

Howard walked back to his desk. He took his bagged lunch out and started eating. The rest of the office crew had already left. As Howard walked by Mags' desk to fill up his water glass, he heard her crying. "Is there anything I can do?" he stopped and asked her.

Mags quickly wiped her eyes. "No, I'm fine."

"If there ever is... you know... anything I can do to help... I'm here," Howard said.

Mags jumped up from her desk and ran to the conference room crying. Howard followed her. "I'm sorry," he said. "I don't know what I did wrong."

"It's not you, Howard," Mags turned around to face him. "It's just... I can't tell you, you will think I'm crazy. Lisa already thinks I'm losing my mind. I don't know. Maybe I am."

"I know you are not crazy. You are an intelligent young woman," Howard said as he sat down at the conference table. "That wasn't much of a compliment, was it? I'm not very good at this."

"Good at what?" Mags asked.

"Talking to girls, young women, you know, ladies," Howard said, looking away from her.

"I think you do just fine. And thank you for the compliment," Mags smiled.

"How about lunch? I have an extra sandwich," Howard asked.

"Sure, why not," Mags answered, with a not so excited tone.

Howard went back to his desk and got his bagged lunch. He had packed an extra sandwich, hoping for an opportunity to share it with Mags. When the rest of the co-workers came back in the office they could see, through the open door, Howard and Mags sitting at the conference table.

"They look like they are enjoying themselves," Lisa said to Adam. "I wish that relationship would go somewhere. It would be good for both of them."

"Maybe I can expedite matters," Adam told Lisa. Adam stepped to the center of the office and said, rather loudly, "I have an announcement to make."

"Oh no! We lost track of time," Mags said, as she jumped up to clean the conference table.

"Yes. We did," Howard said, smiling, as he folded his paper lunch bag to use again the next day.

Mags hurried back to her desk as Adam continued with his announcement, "I am having a cookout at my house tonight. Everyone is invited."

"Oh good! Now, what will I wear? Will there be music and dancing?" Kelly asked as she twirled around.

"Of course, there will be," Adam laughed.

"I'll be there," Tom said as he took Kelly's hand and twirled her again.

Howard walked over to Mags' desk. "How about it, Mags? Its sounds like fun. Will you go?"

"Yes! She's going," Lisa spoke up. "As a matter of fact, we're leaving from work early, to go buy her something to wear."

"What? No, Lisa. I can't," Mags started to protest.

"You can and you will. I don't have any appointments for the rest of the day. Now, get your bag and let's go." Lisa turned and winked at Howard. He smiled knowing she was trying to help him win Mags' heart.

Later that evening, Lisa and Mags walked through the gates to Adam's back yard. The sun had set and the stars were shining in the night sky. Mags felt as though she had stepped into a wonderland. Lights twinkled in all the trees, across the wooden fence and on the back of the house.

As she stood there, with the breeze gently blowing her long flowing dress against her legs, she saw the gazebo. Now, she knew she must be in a fairytale. As the music quietly played in the background, the tiny lights that hung from the rails and the roof of the gazebo flashed in sequence.

Howard was standing by the outdoor kitchen when he caught a glimpse of the woman he loved. Her hair was long and loose, instead of pinned up as she wore it every day. He had never seen her look so feminine, so soft, so beautiful.

As Howard started to walk toward Mags, mesmerized by her beauty, Kelly came running up to her. "Wow! Look at our little Mags! All dressed up and ready to party!"

Howard quickly turned and walked to the grill where Adam and Lisa were watching. "Turn the music up," Adam said to Lisa. "I've chosen all slow dance songs for tonight. We have your back, buddy," Adam said to Howard.

Tom came through the gates and grabbed ahold of Kelly's hands, swinging her around. "Let's get this party started!" he said.

As the wine bottle was being opened and poured, Adam called to Mags, "Hey, Mags! I have some hot tea, just for you."

"Thank you. That was very thoughtful," Mags said as she walked over to them.

After she poured hot water over the teabag in the cup Howard said to her, "It's a beautiful night."

"Yes, it is," Mags said as she was looking at the lights again. "It's, almost, as though the stars have come down from heaven and have surrounded us."

Howard set his wineglass down on the counter. He took a step closer to Mags, who was still looking up at the stars. "Could I...?"

Before he could finish his question, Adam announced, "Dinner is ready! Grab a plate and dig in."

Howard watched Mags as she walked back to the gazebo, alone. "Now's your chance," Lisa said, pushing him. "Everyone is eating. You have her and the dancefloor all to yourself."

As Howard walked up to Mags, she was standing on the dancefloor in the gazebo, her head leaned back and her eyes closed. "I just don't know what's real, anymore," she said quietly to herself.

"I do," Howard said, as he stepped up onto the dancefloor.

"Oh! I didn't know anyone was there!" Mags was startled by him.

"I'm here and I'm real," Howard said stepping closer to her.

"Why do you keep saying that?" Mags asked tearfully.

"Saying what?" Howard replied.

"You keep saying 'I'm here.' Ever since I got the flowers. The flowers! They weren't from him…they were from…" She stopped speaking.

"I brought you the flowers. I thought you would like them," Howard said.

"So, he's not here? He's not… real?" she said quietly.

"Who, what, are you talking about?" Howard was trying to understand her.

"Shh. Listen." Mags held her hand up to stop him from talking. "I love this song."

Howard reached out for Mags' hand. She put her hand in his and they stepped to the middle of the dancefloor. As they, very slowly, swayed around the gazebo, Howard sang, very quietly, to Mags,

"Looking back on the memory of
The dance we shared beneath the stars above
For a moment all the world was right."

Mags laid her head on Howard's chest and he held her tightly as they danced. "All the world is right," Howard said to her.

"Who would have thought it would take Garth Brooks' song 'The Dance' to bring these two together?" Lisa said as they all watched the relationship between Howard and Mags blossom.

"Why can't you just be him?" Mags whispered.

"Maybe I am," Howard said.

As the song ended, so did the dance. The couple stood, awkwardly, for an instant, still on the dancefloor with their arms around each other. Then Mags took a step back and looked at Howard. He simply smiled at her. She looked down at the floor. "I don't know what to do," she said.

"Then don't 'do' anything," Howard said, picking her chin up so he could look her in her eyes, "just let it happen."

Chapter 11

"Flowers in the Hair"

Days had passed by since the dance at Adam's cookout. Howard and Mags had lunch together at the conference table every day. But on this one day, Howard seemed especially nervous. He dropped nearly everything he touched. He knocked over Mags' glass of water. "I'm so sorry, Mags," he said as he wiped it up.

"What is wrong with you today, Howard? You are awfully jumpy," Mags said.

"Nothing is wrong. Everything is fine. I just... well... I wanted to ask you..." as he spoke these words, the rest of the office crew came through the door returning from lunch.

"Well, try to calm down before you break something," Mags said as she got up to go back to work.

Howard stayed to himself the rest of the day. At the end of the workday Howard approached Adam, "When are you having another cookout?"

Lisa was standing by Adam when Howard asked. She quietly said to Adam, "I don't think he's as interested in the food as he is in the other guests. Or should we say 'guest'?"

"I notice there has been a daily lunch date in the conference room lately," Lisa said to Howard.

"Hey, everybody!" Adam said loudly as Howard stepped away so Mags wouldn't become suspicious. I'm having another cookout at my house tonight. And yes, Kelly, there will be dancing."

"Woohoo!" Kelly cheered.

Tom walked over to Adam saying, "Sounds like fun. Kelly and I will bring the steaks this time."

"I'll bring the wine," Lisa added.

Adam looked at Mags, "How about it, Mags, are you coming?"

"I would love to come. What do you want me to bring?" Mags said.

Lisa looked at Mags, "You just wear that beautiful dress you wore the last time and enjoy yourself. We have everything taken care of."

Later that evening, when it was about time to leave for the cookout, Lisa knocked on Mags' door. Mags opened the door looking more beautiful than ever. "Why Mags, I do believe you are wearing the lip-gloss I made you buy when you bought the dress," Lisa said.

"Are you ready?" Mags asked.

"I am. But you're not. Not quite, anyway," Lisa said handing her a bunch of baby's breath flowers. "For your hair."

Mags sat down on the couch and Lisa put flowers in her long, wavy, blonde hair, one by one.

"Why are you going to so much trouble for me, Lisa?" Mags asked.

"Because you deserve it! Tonight is your night to be a princess," Lisa said.

"How do I look?" Mags stood up when Lisa had finished putting the flowers in her hair.

"Stunning! Absolutely, stunning! Like a princess should look," Lisa answered her. "Come on. Let's get going. We don't want them to start the party without us," Lisa said as they started toward the door.

When they arrived at Adam's house, the music was already playing and the food was on the grill. Adam took the wine from Lisa and said, "Oh good, already chilled. Mags, I have hot tea for you."

"Thanks Adam," she said as she walked around the yard looking up at the night sky and all the twinkling lights around her. Mags went to her favorite place to watch the lights, the gazebo. As she stood there, she gazed out into the wonders of the heavens, looking as if she were a million miles and a lifetime away.

Howard immediately went to her. He stepped up on the dancefloor, breaking her concentration. "Another beautiful night," he said.

"Just perfect. As perfect as the first time I ever saw this place," Mags said.

"I hope tonight will be even more perfect for you, Mags," Howard said.

"Howard, I want to tell you something." Mags looked at him. "I'm really happy that we are friends now. Even the office crew. I feel like we are all friends, and I like that."

Adam had just pulled the steaks off the grill and was about to announce that dinner was ready, when Lisa stopped him.

"Look," she said. "I think they should be alone."

Just then, Tom, and Kelly walked up. "Shh," Lisa made sure they didn't say a word.

Howard put his hand in his pocket. "I was thinking Mags, well... I thought..." He pulled a small box out of his pocket. Mags was looking at the stars again and didn't see what he was doing.

"Just look at those stars. They make you feel like anything is possible. There are no boundaries, no limits. That is, if you love enough. Don't you think so Howard?" Mags looked back at Howard.

He opened the box revealing a ring, dropped to one knee and said, "Yes, I do believe anything is possible."

"Howard! What are you doing? Get up. Is this some kind of joke? Did they put you up to it?" She looked over at the outdoor kitchen to see if the office crew was watching. To her surprise, no one was there. Adam, Lisa, Tom and Kelly had slipped away. They had gone inside to give Howard and Mags some privacy.

Howard stood up. "This is not a joke, Mags."

"Well, what then? You're really asking me to marry you?" Mags asked.

"Yes Mags! I'm asking you to marry me. Is that so hard to believe? I love you Mags," Howard said.

"Howard, don't. Just... don't. We barely know each other," Mags said walking to the other side of the gazebo.

Howard followed her, "Mags, you know everything there is to know about me. I have shown you every side of my personality. And I have felt like I have known the real you, ever since the day I found your journal on the floor."

Mags turned toward him, "You found my journal on the floor?"

"Yes, it had fallen out of your bag as you were leaving work. I put it in your desk drawer," Howard said.

"How did that make you feel like you know me better? Howard, did you read my journal!?!" Mags was getting angrier by the second.

"It fell open when it hit the floor. Yes, I read a few pages. Mags, I couldn't help myself. Your expressions of love touched my heart so deeply that I just knew it had to be about me. That was the only part I read. I wanted to let you know, I'm here for you. On any level you want, a secret admirer, a lunch buddy, a dance partner and yes, even a husband."

Mags was livid as she said, "Those words were not meant to be read by anyone, ever!"

"I am so sorry, Mags. Please, will you forgive me?" Howard begged her.

"You tricked me, Howard. You made me think that somehow, you were him. That's why I haven't dreamed about him lately. I have been letting my thoughts and feelings get confused by you," she said as she walked across the gazebo.

"Dream? What do you mean dream? You mean I've been competing with a figment of your imagination?" Howard asked.

"He is real to me," Mags replied.

"Mags, you have to have some feelings for me," Howard followed her again. "Remember the dance? Right here on this dancefloor? You felt so right in my arms."

"It was the wine, Howard," Mags retorted.

"Mags, you didn't have any wine. Those were real feelings. You will never convince me differently."

"Well, even if that is true, they are gone now. And so am I. Tell Lisa that I am taking a cab home." Mags walked away from the gazebo, pulling the flowers out of her hair and throwing them down. "Princess, huh," she said as she opened the gate and walked through it.

The rest of the office crew came out of the house. "What happened? Where is Mags?" Lisa asked.

"She said to tell you she is taking a cab home, Lisa." Howard was still standing on the dancefloor with the ring in his hand. He closed the box, put it back in his pocket and said, "I'm leaving, too. See you tomorrow." By the time he had gotten to the front yard, Mags was gone.

Lisa said to Adam, "Well, thanks for trying. I better go check on her."

"What happened? Did I miss something?" Kelly asked.

"Kelly, you always miss something. How about we eat," Tom said.

"Let me know if you need anything," Adam said to Lisa.

Lisa got to the apartment building and knocked on Mags' door. "Mags, it's Lisa. Let me in," she said.

"No. I just want to be alone," Mags answered her.

"I just want to make sure you are alright," Lisa asked.

Mags opened the door. "Did you know?"

"Did I know what?" Lisa asked as she walked in.

"Did you know that Howard read my journal?" Mags asked.

Lisa had stepped into the kitchen to make Mags a cup of tea. She stepped back into the living room where Mags had sat down. "No! He read your journal?"

"He read my most private and intimate thoughts and feelings," Mags cried.

"Oh, honey. I am so sorry," Lisa said as Mags laid her head on her shoulder and sobbed.

"Do you think maybe, just maybe, you could forgive him?" Lisa asked. "I am sure he really cares about you."

"Forgive him?" Mags sat up. "It was all fake. It was all based on his misconception that I was writing in my journal about him. No. I don't even want to forgive him. I just want to get my Jess back."

"Jess," Lisa said quietly. "I thought we had moved past Jess."

Just then the tea kettle whistled. "I'll get your tea for you," Lisa said.

"I'll never move past my Jess, never," Mags said to herself.

"Why don't you go wash your face and put on your pajamas while I make your tea?" Lisa asked. "You don't want to fall asleep in that beautiful dress and ruin it."

"Why not," Mags said as she did what Lisa asked. "I'm never wearing it again."

When Mags came back out of the bedroom with her face washed and wearing her pajamas, Lisa had her hot cup of tea waiting for her on the coffee table. "Do you want me to stay the night here with you? I can just run next door and get my things."

Mags took a few sips of the tea and calmed down. "No, Lisa. I'll be fine."

"Are you sure?" Lisa asked again. "I don't mind at all."

"I know you are always here when I need you, Lisa. You are the best big sister in the world." Mags smiled. "But really, go on to your apartment. I'll be fine."

"Alright, if you are sure. Just remember, I'm right next door if you need me," Lisa said as she walked to the apartment door.

"I'll remember. Good night, Lisa," Mags said as she got up to lock the door behind Lisa. Then she finished her tea and put the cup in the sink. She quickly went to bed so sure that she would reunite with her love, Jess, in her dreams.

The next few days were grueling for Mags. There was no Jess in her dreams, and she had no Howard paying attention to her at work. He seemed to avoid her and ignore her on every possible occasion. But that was fine with Mags. She was still mad at him for, what she thought was, tricking her.

Chapter 12

"Left Alone"

Lisa called the office staff into an unexpected meeting. "As you all know, the boss has been away more than usual lately. Well, we have a big surprise for all of you! Monitek is expanding!"

Lisa opened the conference room door. As they walked in they were all shocked! Lisa had gotten in early and had filled the room with balloons and streamers. On the conference table, very organized, in front of each person's chair, were party hats and horns. In the middle of the table was a cake from the best bakery in town.

"Congratulations to Monitek!!!" was written on it. Beside the table was a bucket of ice with a bottle of champagne chilling.

Everyone took their assigned seats. There was chatter and mumbling as they all looked at each other curiously, wondering what the future held in store for them.

Lisa stepped to the head of the table. Seeing that no one was paying attention to her, she tapped her pen on the side of her glass. The room became silent. "We, that is, the boss and I, are opening another office!"

Adam spoke up, "What does that mean for all of us? Are any of us being transferred?"

"What?" Howard seemed shaken by that word.

"Transferred? Forget about that. Are we getting raises?" Tom asked.

"We certainly deserve raises!" Kelly chimed in.

"Everyone! Please, just hold on. I will try to explain things to you step by step." Lisa took a deep breath, as she knew this next point would not be taken well. "No raises, not quite yet anyway."

The mumbling and chatter began again. "But no transfers either," Lisa started talking louder until the chatter stopped. "This leads me to my next point. As office manager and assistant to the boss—"

Kelly interrupted her, "Oh here we go again. You don't have to remind us about who runs the office, Lisa."

As Adam and Tom snickered, Lisa continued speaking, "As I was saying, we are opening a new office, and the boss wants me to meet him there to get it set up. I will be doing the interviews for the hiring of the new staff. He wanted me to be sure to express his pride and gratitude to all of you for making the company such a complete success! Because of this, he is giving all of you four days off... WITH PAY!"

This news was met with a round of applause and cheers. Everyone was extremely happy and excited to have extra paid vacation time. Everyone except Mags. She had been sitting quietly in her chair listening to all the excitement surrounding her; but feeling nothing.

"I will be leaving Friday, tomorrow, after work and I will return next Friday. I expect everyone to be back in the office next Friday ready to go back to work. I am sure we will have much to catch up on."

Lisa stepped back and picked up the bottle of champagne. "But for now," she popped the cork and champagne spewed all over, "let's party!"

"Mags," Lisa said as she poured the champagne, "I was thinking. Why don't you come with me on the trip? We will have the weekend to do some sightseeing before I start the interviews on Monday. And you can help me with the shopping to decorate the office."

"Thanks, Lisa. I really appreciate it. But I think I'll just stay home and get some rest. Maybe I'll work on my book. I'm almost at the end. Besides, you're the shopper and decorator, not me."

Howard had cut the cake and passed it around. He put a large piece in front of Mags. Kelly looked at him and shook her head, "You just don't give up, do you?"

Without a word, Mags picked up her plate and started to leave the room. "If you change your mind let me know. It could be like old times in the college dorms," Lisa said.

Mags smiled at Lisa and took her cake back to her desk. She could hear all her co-workers laughing and talking from the conference room. They were all making plans for what they were going to do on their unexpected paid days off.

Howard was the first of them to come out of the conference room. As he walked past her, Mags looked up. She didn't mean for it to happen, but their eyes met. Still raw from being hurt, Howard felt embarrassed that he had even looked her way. He was even a little bit mad with her but mostly he was heartbroken. He quickly looked away and went to his desk.

Mags instinctively took out her journal and started writing. "I have one week, seven days, to get back to him. I don't care what it takes or what I have to do. I must get back to him!"

She looked up and around to make sure no one was watching her. She was safe from glaring eyes so she continued writing. "I am dying here without him! I can't go on any longer. Without hearing his voice, seeing his smile, looking into his eyes, and feeling his touch I will simply cease to exist."

Mags stopped writing long enough to wipe the tears from her face. Then she picked her pen up again. "This is my last chance. There will be no one here to interrupt me. I'll give it my all even if I end up with nothing. I will get back to him... or die trying."

Mags only had this one night to prepare. She planned to hunker down in her apartment. Mags was determined she would not come out until she was with Jess... or she would not come out.

At the end of the day, Lisa told the office crew, "I'll be leaving the first thing in the morning. Please make sure you complete all of your work tomorrow before you start enjoying your days off."

Kelly spoke up, "We're not in high school, Lisa."

"Well, sometimes you act like you are, Kelly," Adam laughed.

Lisa asked her friend again, "Mags please, will you reconsider and go with me on the trip? You can relax by the pool, sleep all day, whatever you want to do. You don't have to go shopping with me or anything."

Mags just shook her head.

"I have a bad feeling about this," Lisa said.

"A bad feeling about what?" Mags asked, worried that Lisa had somehow figured out what she was planning.

"I have a bad feeling about leaving you alone for a week. I'm afraid you will hold up in your apartment and get so lost in your writing that you forget to eat or anything." Lisa was truly concerned about her lifelong friend.

Mags said, "I promise I will not get lost in my writing. I will get supplies, I will make sure I have everything that I need. Don't worry about me, Lisa. I know what I have to do."

As everyone else was leaving for the day, Howard walked by Mags as she was picking up her bag. He paused for an instant. He didn't even look her way. He just said, quietly, to himself, "Oh, what could have been. If only..." Then he walked out of the office.

As Lisa was locking the door, Mags stopped and turned back toward her. "I really do love you, Lisa. You do know that, right? You are my sister, no matter what."

Lisa closed the door behind them. "Of course, I know that, Mags. I love you, too." She had color swatches in her hand. "Hey, what color do you think I should choose for the new office? Matching ours or should I go totally different?"

Mags just hugged her friend and said, "You're the one with the good taste. You will do a great job. You always have." Lisa was too preoccupied with work to see the tears in her friend's eyes.

Both young women walked away, going in very different directions, in many ways. Mags went to the corner drugstore and bought sleeping pills. Then she went to another drugstore, so as not to raise any suspension, and bought more sleeping pills. Then another store and another.

Mags got back to her apartment and made sure she locked the door. Then she went into the kitchen with all the supplies she had bought, all sleeping pills. As she opened the bottles, one after the other, she poured the pills into a bowl. Then she got a glass of water and started to drink and swallow pills. Not too many, not at first, anyway. Just a few to help her get into that deep sleep. That place where she could find her Jess.

Mags put the glass of water and the bowl of sleeping pills on the coffee table. Then she got her journal out of her bag and sat down on her couch. She was reading passages she had written over the past few weeks when she drifted off to sleep.

Chapter 13

"It will End"

Jess found Magnolia sitting on the beach staring out over the ocean. "I've been looking for you everywhere. I thought we were going hiking this morning, on the other side of the island?" he said to her.

"I couldn't go," was all she said. She never even looked at him.

"Magnolia, what's wrong?" Jess sat down beside her.

"I don't know. But it's… well… I can't explain it, Jess." Magnolia looked at him with tears streaming down her face.

"That's alright. We will just sit here together until you do know or until you feel better." Jess put his arm around her and she laid her head on his shoulder.

They sat there most of the morning, in the warm sunshine, listening to the calming sound of the waves crashing ashore. "How about if we take a walk together?" Jess spoke up.

She shook her head. "I feel like… like it's not real," Magnolia finally started talking to him.

"You feel like what's not real?" Jess asked, trying to understand her.

"This! All this!" Magnolia motioned around her. "The island! The hurricane! You! I feel like it's all a dream and I'm going to wake up and be in some horrid city, in some miserable life, without you!"

"That's not going to happen," Jess tried to reassure her.

"Since I've been here, on this island, with you, everything seems so perfect. But I keep seeing something different in my mind, in my dreams. I don't know how or why but it's another... another life. I feel like this life, here with you, is somehow just a dream. And I am going to wake up and be in that other life; that life without you, Jess! Without you!"

"We are here! This is now! That's all that matters. Here, feel this," Jess picked up a handful of sand and poured it in her hand. "Do you feel the warmth of the sand? That's real! Come with me."

He took her hand and they walked into the water. "Do you feel that? The coolness of the water splashing against your feet. That's real!"

He took her hand and put it on his chest. "Now, tell me what you feel?" Jess said, very quietly, with tears in his eyes, "What do you feel, Magnolia?"

"I feel your heart beating," she cried.

"Yes, my heart is beating. It is beating for you. I love you, Magnolia. I have loved you ever since I pulled you over the rail on my deck and brought you into the lighthouse. I loved you even before—"

"But it's ending!" she interrupted him. "I feel it. It's ending. And there is nothing we can do to stop it," she could barely speak because she was crying so hard.

Jess took her hand again. "Come with me. There's something I have to show you." He held her hand tightly as he ran back to the lighthouse. She could barely keep up with him. When they got there, he let go of her hand and threw the door open. They both walked inside.

"Here! This is how I know it's all real. This island, the hurricane, my love for you, it's all real. I have always loved you. I have spent years trying to find you. And you finally showed up. Look! This is real!"

He took her to the door that he had told her to never open. It creaked loudly as he pulled on it. The musty smell poured out as he reached in and turned on the light.

Magnolia couldn't believe what she was seeing! She stepped through the doorway to the staircase. "It's me!"

The wall behind the lighthouse stairs was lined with sketches, drawings, paintings... of her!

"I've been seeing you in my dreams for years. I've known for years that I love you. I just had to find you. But when I couldn't, I left civilization and found this island. That's why I moved here, to restore this lighthouse and to work on my drawings and paintings. I had to get away from the daily reminders that I didn't have the woman I loved by my side. And then you came! You found me! You are here and I love you. Yes, Magnolia! This is real!"

She started to climb the wobbly staircase looking at each drawing. The detail, the accuracy, was incredible. One step after another, one picture after another, she stopped and took it all in. "I don't understand," she stopped and looked back at him, "I just don't understand."

"You came to me with no memory. I didn't question you. Now I ask you not to question me. I don't know how I have seen you in my dreams, but I have. And through all the years of my friends dating, getting married, and having families it became clear to me that I would only ever love you."

At the top of the lighthouse staircase was a canvas painting that she was climbing up to see. "Magnolia, don't go any higher. The steps aren't sturdy!" Jess warned her. But she knew she had to get a closer look at the painting. It was a painting of her sitting on a suitcase in front of a building.

"Jess! I understand now. I know this building. I remember this place. That's why you have dreamed of me.

You have seen me. Jess, this is the Brownstone Tudor where I live! This was the day I moved in. I remember that I didn't have the key to my apartment so I had to wait outside. The moving van had the street blocked and traffic had to stop. Jess! I remember! A taxicab stopped in front of my apartment building, next to where I was sitting on my suitcase. I looked toward the cab. I saw a young man sleeping. Then he woke up and looked at me. He smiled just as the cab driver pulled away."

Jess climbed a few steps toward her, "I remember that day! That was when I started to dream about you. But it wasn't a dream! I haven't been just dreaming about you. I've been remembering you, Magnolia!"

"As your cab pulled away, Lisa, drove up. Lisa! My sister! Jess, I have a sister! I remember now! I remember everything!"

Just as Magnolia spoke those words, the step she was standing on began to crack. Jess yelled out to her as he ran up the staircase, "Come back down!" Suddenly, there was a loud crack and the step she was standing on broke from under her feet!

"No!" Jess screamed as the woman he loved fell from the top of the lighthouse stairs! Jess ran back down the stairs to her. He threw the collapsed steps and railing away from on top of her. "Magnolia, speak to me," Jess pleaded as he pulled her close to him.

Her eyes opened and she smiled, "By the way. I love you, too." Then her eyes closed and her body went limp.

Jess lifted Magnolia gently from the rubble and carried her to the couch. He laid her head softly on a pillow and covered her with a blanket. "Magnolia, please wake up," he begged. He could tell she was still breathing although it seemed difficult for her.

Jess grabbed the radio microphone. "Hello tower. This is Jess. Is anyone there?"

"Hey, Jess. This is Joe. I was about to call you. We have that information you were looking for about the missing girl. Her sister put out a missing person report on her when she didn't check in on schedule."

"Not now Joe! I have an emergency! I need the rescue helicopter sent from the mainland immediately!"

"Sure thing, Jess," Joe replied. "Calling now."

Jess got a cloth, wet it, and wiped Magnolia's face. Her eyes opened briefly. "Jess, I remember," she said as her eyes closed again.

"Stay with me, Magnolia! Help is on the way," Jess held her hand and talked to her hoping she could hear him.

"The voice on the radio quickly replied, "Jess, chopper is in the air. Whatever has happened, I hope they get there in time."

Jess didn't even let go of Magnolia's hand to answer the radio call. Magnolia came to again, just as Jess heard the helicopter overhead. "The book, get me the book, Jess. It's important," she said to him.

He put her hand down and ran into the bedroom. He picked up the mysterious journal from the top of the dresser where Magnolia had put it. She never had opened it. She was too afraid of what it might contain. He ran back to her and put it in her hand.

At that moment, the paramedics banged on the door. "In here!" Jess yelled. "We're in here."

Magnolia was having more difficulty breathing. They put oxygen on her and hooked her up to an I.V. solution of saline. "It looks like she may have a concussion and some broken ribs. That's why she's having trouble breathing."

The paramedics put her on a stretcher and hurried to get her back to the helicopter waiting for them on the beach. They loaded her up and told Jess, "Get in. We will have her at the hospital in ten minutes."

Jess yelled to the pilot, "Radio Joe. Tell him to contact her sister and have her meet us at the hospital."

As the helicopter took flight, Jess leaned down close to Magnolia and whispered in her ear. "THIS is 'REALITY'."

Chapter 14

"Too Late?"

Lisa happily strolled into work in the late afternoon on Friday. She had been very successful in setting up the new office for the boss. "I hope everyone enjoyed their time off," she said as she looked around the office.

Everyone was chatting about what they had done while she was away and congratulating her on her accomplishment. "Well, let's get back to work," Lisa said that was enough small talk for this workaholic.

"Were there any important calls, Mags?" Lisa looked toward her friend's desk, but no one was there.

Howard stepped up to Lisa and said, "I thought Mags went with you."

"No. No, she didn't go with me. So, she didn't come in at all today?" Lisa asked.

"Not today. She didn't come in last Friday, either," Howard said. "Has anyone heard from her?"

"Us? Hear from Mags? We are the last people she would call or want to associate with," Kelly said.

"Maybe she just over slept again," Adam added.

"It's 4:00 in the afternoon. That's late, even for Mags," Tom said as he walked over to her desk.

Lisa picked up the phone and called Mags. "No answer," she said.

They all looked at each other, thinking the same thing, but no one said it. Then Howard spoke up, "You don't think—"

Before he could finish his thought, Lisa grabbed her purse and ran for the door. Howard was right on her heals.

Kelly looked at Tom and Adam and said, "Oh no, you don't think..." But, again, no one finished the sentence.

Lisa and Howard ran as fast as they could down the street to the apartment house that Lisa and Mags had lived in since they graduated college. All the while the sound of Mags' voice raced through Lisa's head. "I love you, Lisa," was all she could hear.

It felt to Lisa as if time had stopped and the world was moving in slow motion as they opened the door to the apartment building and headed up the stairs. "Mags! Mags!" Lisa was screaming as they got to her apartment door. They banged on the door. "Mags, open the door! It's Lisa!" she cried out.

"Do you have a key?" Howard asked Lisa.

"Yes! In my apartment." She hurried to her apartment to get the key. Howard continued beating on the door and calling for Mags to come and open it.

Lisa came running back with the key. "Please no! Please no!" Lisa kept repeating over and over. Her hands shook so badly that she couldn't get the key in the lock.

"Here, let me," Howard took the key from her and unlocked the door. He pushed the door open and Lisa ran in.

"No!" she screamed as her worst fears were realized!

"Mags... no..." Lisa dropped to her knees beside the couch. There was her lifelong best friend, her adopted sister, her "Mags," unconscious on the couch with her journal in her hand and sleeping pills spilled on the coffee table.

Howard was already calling the paramedics as Lisa tried to wake her. "Is she...?" he started to say as he hung up the phone.

"She is breathing, but just barely." Lisa kept shaking her, "Why, Mags, why?" Lisa cried.

Howard wet a cloth and wiped her face with it. Lisa kept calling her name and trying to wake her friend. The paramedics arrived and did all they could to stabilize Mags. They put her on oxygen and hooked her up to an I.V. solution. But when they looked in her eyes with a flashlight, Lisa heard one of the paramedics say, "No, response. Let's go." Immediately, they took her on the stretcher from the apartment to the waiting rescue unit.

Lisa picked up Mags journal from the floor where it had fallen when she was trying to make her wake up. She held it tightly to her chest. "My car is parked outside," Lisa said to Howard. "You will have to drive, I can't... I just can't..." Lisa couldn't finish her statement. She just handed Howard the keys. They ran out the door just after the paramedics. They didn't even pause to close the apartment door.

The stretcher carrying the one person they both dearly loved was lifted into the rescue ambulance. As soon as the doors closed, the sirens came on and the ambulance took off. Within seconds, Mags was on her way to, at least in Lisa's eyes, lifesaving treatment.

During the drive to the hospital, Lisa kept saying to herself, "Why didn't I listen. Why didn't I just listen."

Howard never spoke, not a single word. The drive to the hospital only took ten minutes in actual time. But to Howard and Lisa, it felt like hours!

When they arrived at the nurses' station, they were told that Mags had been taken to the I.C.U. Howard and Lisa were asked to make themselves comfortable in the waiting room until the doctor came to talk to them.

They both took seats that faced the double doors to the corridor that led to the area where Mags was being treated. Lisa, still clutching Mags' journal tightly to her heart, crumpled over in her chair crying. Howard sat and stared at the door, as if his thoughts, feelings, and hopes could penetrate the walls and help his true love.

When he realized that Lisa was falling apart, he reached over to her and put his hand on her shoulder, "We have to be strong for her, because she can't be strong for herself right now." Lisa, sat up and nodded her head in agreement.

After what seemed like an eternity for these two, one of the doctors treating Mags came into the I.C.U. waiting room. "I'm looking for the family of Mag—" he didn't even finish saying her name before Lisa and Howard jumped up from the chairs they had been sitting in.

"How is she?" Lisa immediately asked.

"Are you family?" the doctor inquired.

"I'm her sister!" Lisa cried.

The doctor looked at Howard, waiting for a reply. Howard reached into his pocket and brought out a small box. With his trembling hand, he held it up to the doctor. With tears in his eyes, Howard simply said, "This was to be hers." He opened the box, revealing a sparkling, diamond ring.

"Sit down. Let's talk," the doctor said to both of them. "I'm going to be straightforward about Magnolia's condition. She has apparently been unconscious for some time. We pumped her stomach but we found no residue of the sleeping pills that the paramedics informed us they believed she had consumed."

"Does that mean Mags didn't take them?" Lisa asked hopefully.

"No, it doesn't mean that at all. It means that she took them long enough ago that they have completely dissolved in her stomach and the effects are now in her system."

Lisa started crying again and Howard tried to console her saying, "Let's hear everything the doctor has to say. Maybe there is something we can do to help."

The doctor waited patiently for Lisa to regain her composure, then he said, "Yes, there is something you can do to help. I need more information to help with her treatment. We need to know, when was the last time anyone had contact with her?"

"I've been out of town for a week," Lisa answered, trying to control her emotions.

"I thought she was with Lisa," Howard added. "So, it's been a week since we saw or talked to her."

"That's about the timeline we thought we were looking at. This is what we have put together from the test results and her condition. In that week, she had nothing to eat and has had very little to drink. With the amount of empty sleeping pill bottles the paramedics found, along with the receipts showing that they were all purchased on the same day, we can only assume that she drank just enough water to swallow the pills."

"Oh, no!" Lisa cried.

"What we can't figure out is this. Why did she space the pills out?" the doctor questioned.

"Do you mean that she didn't take the pills all at once, together? So, she wasn't trying to… to…?" Howard couldn't bring himself to even say the words.

"No, I do not believe she was trying to commit suicide," the doctor replied. "It seems as if she was just trying to sleep. And when I say sleep, I mean sleep for an extended period of time. She was trying to stay asleep without any waking hours."

"Wonderful!" Lisa exclaimed. "That's great news!"

"Hold on now. It's only good news to this point. If she had swallowed that many sleeping pills and had not received any medical assistance right away, we would not even be having this conversation right now."

The doctor shook his head. "But Mags, as you call her, is alive. And she is in for the fight of her life! She is currently on life support. We are just trying to sustain her life right now."

"Can we see her?" Lisa asked through her tears.

"Yes. But remember, she doesn't look like your 'Mags.'" The doctor stood up, "Come this way." Howard and Lisa followed him through those two doors they had been staring at for so long.

When they walked through the glass doors to the room that Mags was being treated in, Lisa became weak from fear and stumbled. Howard caught her and held on to steady her. There was Mags, lying in the hospital bed, hooked up to a machine with a tube going down her throat, taped to her mouth and face. The machine was loud as it breathed for her.

Lines and tubes were everywhere connecting Mags to machines. There were I.V. bags hanging above her, attached with tubes that were giving her life sustaining fluids through her veins.

Lisa stood up straight and stepped toward her friend, "Her coloring... it's so... so grey..."

"That's caused by her body not getting enough oxygen. Even though she was breathing when you found her, there wasn't enough of what she needed to keep her organs functioning. Because of the lack of fluids, her kidneys have now shut down. We can only hope that in the next few hours we can get them functioning again."

"You said lack of oxygen, doctor," Howard asked, "What about her brain? Has her brain been affected?"

"She still has some brain function, but it's too early to know how much or how little," replied the doctor.

Just as Lisa gasped at the thought of Mags coming out of this horror with brain damage, alarms started going off from the heart monitor beside the bed. It was then she realized, Mags might not come out of this at all!

"You will have to leave now!" a nurse was directing Howard and Lisa out of the room as another nurse began doing chest compressions.

"What's that? What does that alarm mean? What's happening?" Lisa begged for answers as the door closed behind them.

"Please wait outside," another nurse said as she walked them back to the waiting room. "Someone will let you know as soon as they can."

Lisa was crying as Howard helped her walk back to the chairs where they had waited earlier. "I have to know, Howard. I have to know why. I need to read her journal. Does that make me a monster?" Lisa asked her companion, taking his mind off his own pain, if only temporarily.

"No, Lisa, it doesn't make you anything but a scared sister. Mags would want you to do whatever it takes for you to get through this. I know she never meant to hurt you. Just don't tell me anything that's in it," Howard told her. "That journal caused me enough grief for a lifetime."

Lisa opened the journal and quickly flipped to the entries Mags made in it on the last day she saw her. She read silently, "I am dying here without him! I can't go on any longer. Without hearing his voice, seeing his smile, looking into his eyes, and feeling his touch I will simply cease to exist. This is my last chance. There will be no one here to interrupt me. I'll give it my all even if I end up with nothing. I will get back to him... or die trying."

"I should never have left her. I should have known," Lisa cried.

"You couldn't have known, Lisa. Please don't blame yourself. If anyone is to blame, it's me. I should have found a way to make her love me. Then this wouldn't be happening. We would be planning our lives together now instead of—" Howard broke down crying.

* * *

When Kelly, Tom and Adam never heard anything from Lisa about Mags, they decided to go by her apartment to check on her. They rode together in Adam's car and parked in front of the Brownstone. "I don't see Lisa's car. Maybe they went out together," Kelly said.

"Let's hope," Adam said as they walked up the stairs.

"Hey! Isn't that Mags' apartment, with the door open?" Tom asked as he looked up the stairs ahead of them.

"Yes, it is," Kelly said, as she ran ahead of the two men. As they caught up to her, they found her standing in Mags' apartment with a horrified look on her face. She held up an empty bottle. "Sleeping pills," she said, "and lots of them."

"I'm calling Lisa," Adam said.

"I'll call Howard," Tom said.

Howard felt his phone vibrate with a call notification. He took it out of his pocket and, without even checking to see who was calling, turned it off.

"No answer," Tom said.

"Me either," said Adam. "Let's go!"

Kelly was the first one down the stairs as they raced to the car to get to the hospital. "I never meant it. It was all in fun. You believe me, don't you?" Kelly was horrified that she had pushed Mags into doing the unthinkable.

"We are just as guilty as you are, Kelly," Tom replied as they all got back in Adam's car.

"No one in this car is innocent. We all had our laughs at Mags' expense and Howard's too," Adam lamented as he drove them to the hospital.

***

The doctor came back out to the waiting room. This time he had a very distressed look on his face as he sat down by Howard and Lisa. "We had you leave the room because Mags' heart stopped beating."

"No!" Lisa screamed. Howard took her hand.

"Wait a minute. She is still alive. We were able to get her heart to start beating again but very slowly. Things don't look good. Her blood pressure is extremely low and her kidneys are still not functioning," the doctor told them.

"When can we see her again?" Howard asked.

"You can come in now. Just remember, if things go badly, you will have to leave the room quickly," the doctor stood up and started to walk with them back to the double doors. He stopped and turned around before they walked through, "If there are any more close family members, you might want to call them now."

"Our parents, but they are out of the country right now," Lisa said as she was starting to shake. Howard put his arm around her and took her to Mags' bedside.

A nurse pulled a chair up for Lisa to sit in. She never noticed that Howard walked to the other side of the bed and took the small box out of his pocket. He opened it and looked at the ring that he had hoped to give to his one true love. He took the ring out of the box and kissed it. With tears in his eyes, he slipped the ring on Mags' left ring finger. Then, he leaned over and kissed her hand.

Lisa had her eyes closed crying and didn't see him, but one of the nurses did. That simple act of love touched this nurse so deeply that she started crying. She had to excuse herself from the room until she could regain her composure.

Suddenly, the alarm went off again. Howard grabbed Lisa by the hand and they ran out of the room and stood just outside the glass wall. The nurses ran in with the crash cart. The doctor followed, not noticing that Howard and Lisa were standing outside the room. "She's in V-fib," the nurse told the doctor.

Howard and Lisa stood there watching the doctor and nurses frantically trying to stabilize Mags' heart with chest compressions and medications. Then they heard the doctor say, "Clear!" They could see the doctor shock her with the defibrillator. Then, the nurses went back to chest compressions.

At that moment, Kelly, Tom, and Adam came up behind them. "How is she?" Adam asked.

Howard just looked at him and slowly shook his head.

Nurses ran in and out of the room with medicine and equipment. They didn't seem to care that the group was standing there.

The doctor shocked her with the defibrillator, "Again!" they could hear him yell, "Again!" The nurses scrambled around Mags, the group standing outside of the glass wall couldn't even see her for all the activity going on in her room.

"I'm so sorry, Lisa! I am so very sorry," Kelly said.

"We are all sorry, Lisa. Howard, please forgive us. We didn't mean any harm," Tom said.

"Is there anything we can do, Lisa?" Adam asked.

Lisa never looked away from Mags' bed, even though she couldn't see her. She kept looking, hoping to catch a glimpse of Mags, hoping she would look at her and smile.

The doctor looked up and saw them all standing outside the glass wall. He walked out to them. "It's as if she has lost all will to live. She has stopped trying. But we won't stop. She is too young to be allowed to give up!"

They all stood silently, watching the nurses push fluids through the I.V. and administering medications through the I.V. The chest compressions continued, as did the defibrillator shocks. Lisa could see Mags' blood pressure numbers dropping steadily.

The doctor came back out and, with tears in his eyes, said, "There is nothing more we can do. Please, come back in. If any of you want to say anything to her, this is the time."

"Can she hear us?" Howard asked.

"Probably not. But it will make her feel better," he said motioning toward Lisa.

Howard and Lisa went in the room and walked over to the bed. The nurses stepped back to give them room.

Kelly, Tom, and Adam went in but stayed back by the wall. Lisa leaned over Mags, her tears dripping onto Mags' cheeks. "To sleep, perchance to dream, my little sister... perchance to dream," she said to her quietly.

"What does that mean?" Tom whispered to Kelly.

"It's Mags' favorite quote from Shakespeare's Hamlet. It means, maybe, she will find peace in death. A peace she couldn't find in life. Because of us, Tom. Because of us," Kelly replied with tears running down her face.

Lisa kissed her sister on the face. Howard held her hand with the ring on it. He leaned in close to her and whispered, "I could have missed the pain, but I'd have had to miss the dance."

As the nurse stepped back over to the bed, she looked at the doctor. He nodded his head. The same nurse that had to leave the room earlier, because she was crying, started turning off the pumps. Tears were streaming down her face as she pushed each button. By the time all the machines were turned off, everyone in the room was quietly sobbing.

"We have never seen a case so gut wrenchingly sad and frustrating! I am so sorry we couldn't help her," the doctor said to Lisa. "You take all the time you want with your sister." The doctor and the nurses all left the room.

"We will leave you alone, too," Adam said as he, Tom, and Kelly walked out to the waiting room.

"I'll go too," Howard said.

"No," Lisa looked at him, "please stay with me." She reached her hand out to him. Howard walked over beside Lisa and put his arm around her. Lisa laid her head on his shoulder. "I never knew how much I depended on her. I'm alone now, Howard. I'm all alone."

"No, you're not alone. You have me, Lisa. You have me," Howard said.

After a while, Lisa said, "It's time. Let's go now," and they walked outside the room. They stopped just past the door as the nurses went back in. Lisa watched as they pulled the sheet up over her Mags. Then she turned and they walked out.

Chapter 15

"Our Lighthouse"

The helicopter landed on the roof of the hospital. What seemed like a swarm of nurses and doctors were waiting and ready to take Magnolia in. As they ran with her on the gurney, Jess stayed right by her side. When they ran through the waiting room, one of the nurses stopped Jess and said, "You will have to wait here."

"But…" he started to say something but then he realized that Magnolia getting treatment was far more important than him knowing what was going on.

"Someone will be out to let you know how she is as soon as we can," the nurse said as she ran off.

The pilot found Jess, "I just wanted to let you know, we heard back from Joe. He contacted the sister. She's flying in."

"Thank you," Jess said, "I appreciate everything you have done."

They shook hands and the pilot left. Now all Jess could do was wait…and think. "Will she be alright? Now that she remembers who she is, will she want to leave the island and go back to her old life? Will she want to leave me?" He had so many questions running through his head.

After what seemed to Jess like an eternity, the doctor came out to talk to him. "Are you the one who brought Magnolia in?" he asked Jess.

"Yes, I'm Jess. How is she?" Jess asked as he stood up.

"She has some broken ribs. That's why she was having trouble breathing. But she also has a very serious concussion. That is why she was in and out of consciousness."

"Will she be alright?" Jess interrupted the doctor.

"She will need a lot of rest, but she should be fine. But our tests show that she recently had another concussion. Do you know anything about that?" the doctor asked him.

"Yes, she was in a boat, offshore, when the hurricane hit. She lost her boat and washed up onshore on my island. She didn't know how long she was unconscious before she woke up on the beach. She found my lighthouse when the storm caught up to her and the island," Jess explained to the doctor.

"How was she affected by the first concussion?" the doctor asked.

"She had no memory of who she was or where she came from. She only knew that her name was Magnolia. We pieced together part of what happened from the debris that washed ashore. Then we found a dry box that was definitely hers so we were sure she had been on a boat that went down in the ocean," Jess said as he sat back down.

"It wasn't until she saw the painting in the lighthouse that she remembered who she was and where she came from." Jess continued, "that was when she fell. I should have fixed those steps before now."

"She is going to recover, so you don't need to beat yourself up over what happened. What painting brought back her memory?" the doctor asked.

"It seems that, several years ago, I saw her. She was just sitting on her suitcase in front of her apartment building, waiting to move in. It's funny, for all these years, I thought I dreamed her up. But there she is, flesh and blood. Real. Anyway, I have been drawing and painting pictures of her. I showed her the painting of that day and, all at once, she remembered everything. She was so excited! Then it happened! The steps broke, and she fell from the top of the staircase." Jess stood back up. "I'll never forgive myself if—"

The doctor interrupted him, "Stop worrying, she will be fine. That's the same story she told me. It's so incredible that I just had to hear it from you too."

"When can I see her?" Jess asked.

"You can see her now. She has been asking for you. Just follow me." The doctor walked him to Magnolia's room.

"Jess!" Magnolia smiled and reached her hand out to him.

"Magnolia, I was so worried. I would never have forgiven myself if anything—" Magnolia put her fingers on his lips.

"Shhh, I'm going to be fine. The doctor said so. I just have to rest and let these ribs heal, and get rid of this headache," she laughed. "Oh, now that hurt."

"How about if we just sit here quietly for now?" Jess asked her taking her hand to hold.

"But I remember now. I have to tell you... everything!" she said excitedly.

"We have plenty of time for that. Right now, you need quiet and rest," Jess said.

"Will you do one thing for me?' Magnolia asked Jess.

"I will do anything for you. What do you want?" he replied.

"My journal is on the table over there. Will you get it for me?" she asked him.

Jess walked over to the table and picked up the journal. "You know, just a few days ago, you were afraid of what was in here."

"That was because I didn't know. Now I remember. Jess, open it and start reading it to me. My eyes are blurry."

"Blurry? I'll get the doctor," Jess said as he rushed to the door.

"No, Jess. They said it's from the concussion. My vision will be back to normal in no time. Just read to me please."

Jess pulled a chair over to her bedside. He opened the journal and started reading to her:

Later that day at the office, the coworkers were making plans, almost a daily ritual for this group. 'Lisa, we're going out for drinks after work. Are you in?' Tom asked her, walking by Mags desk without even looking her way.

"Yeah, and maybe a little dancing," Kelly chimed in, taking Tom's hand and starting to spin around.

"Alright people, remember this is an office, not a nightclub," Lisa spoke up.

"Right, this is not the club. It has better music!" Adam, the only over 30-year-old in this group of 20 somethings, laughed, "So, is that a yes, Lisa?"

"Of course, I'll be there." Lisa answered.

Tom looked at Mags, "What about you, Miss Mags? Do you want to go out with the office crew tonight?"

Howard, the accounts manager, stood up and took a step toward the group. He knew how this scene was about to play out. He had witnessed it many times, but he could never muster up the strength to speak out to stop it. Once again, his own shyness overtook him and he turned and sat back down; disappointed in himself.

"No, thank you," Mags couldn't stand these people. They liked to party, a lot, and in her opinion the whole group was loud and obnoxious; except for Lisa, she was Mags' one and only true friend.

Kelly walked over to Mags and, looking straight at her said, "Poor Mags can't go out and have a good time. She has to go home and feed her cat, or is it cats?" The whole group laughed; Lisa didn't think it was funny.

She looked at the group that now encircled Mags' desk, like vultures waiting for their prey, they awaited the next joke. "If Mags doesn't want to go, she doesn't want to go. Leave her alone and get back to work everybody!" They all walked away and Mags smiled at her friend. "Besides, you don't even have a cat," Lisa said quietly and they both laughed.

After reading a few pages of her journal, Jess looked at Magnolia, "This isn't a journal at all. This is a novel you are writing."

"Exactly. That's why I took the boat out. I needed to be alone to finish writing it. When my memory started trying to come back, what I thought were visions of 'reality,' were just glimpses of memories of what I was writing. I was so involved in my book, before the storm, that it became my 'reality.' So, as I started to remember, that was what I was remembering, my novel. I wasn't remembering my real life with my sister and my friends at work. Oh! My sister, Lisa! I have to call Lisa! She must be worried sick. I missed my check in time."

Jess tried to calm her, "It's alright, Magnolia. I sent her a message. She is flying in."

"Oh, thank you, Jess," she said as she was grabbing her head.

"You have to rest now," Jess said as he put the book down.

The nurse came in the room, "How is our island girl feeling?"

"Her head is hurting pretty bad," Jess answered for her.

"I can give her something to help with that. Then we will need to turn the lights down so she can get some rest."

"I'll go back to the waiting room so you can sleep," Jess started to get up from the chair.

"No!" Magnolia said as she grabbed his hand, "don't leave me."

"Well, it looks like you will be staying," the nurse laughed.

Jess sat back down beside Magnolia and held her hand while the nurse administered the medication. As she walked to the door and turned off the overhead light, she stopped and said, "All I can say is that you both will have quite a story to tell your children and grandchildren." Jess and Magnolia both smiled.

Magnolia slept for quite a while with Jess' head laying on the bed beside her. Then the door to the room opened.

"Magnolia?" a voice said in the dimly lit room.

"Lisa? Lisa, is that you? Turn the light on," Magnolia said as she and Jess woke up.

Lisa turned the light on and ran to her sister and hugged her. "Easy Lisa, broken ribs here," Magnolia said.

"I was so worried. How are you? Will you be alright?" Lisa was frantically asking.

"I'm fine, Lisa. I'm fine, really," Magnolia said as she motioned for Jess to come back to her bedside. He had walked away to give Lisa room. "I want you to meet Jess. He saved me."

Lisa and Jess shook hands, "I can't thank you enough for helping my little sister. Our parents died in a car crash when Magnolia was 16 years old. I was 25. I've been taking care of her ever since then," Lisa said. "Magnolia, the office crew is here."

"Everybody? They flew in with you?" Magnolia asked.

"Of course, they did! We all love our Magnolia," Lisa answered her. "Do you feel like seeing them?"

"Oh yes, I do! I want them to meet Jess, too."

Lisa went to the door, opened it and motioned for them. Howard, Kelly, Tom, and Adam all walked in. Kelly went over to Magnolia and gave her a very gentle hug.

"We were so worried about you. Don't you ever disappear like that again!" Kelly said.

"Let me introduce everyone. This is my best friend, next to my sister of course, Kelly," Magnolia announced.

Tom walked over and shook Jess' hand and said, "I hear we are in your debt for saving our little Magnolia."

Adam was next to shake his hand, "Yes, the nurses are all talking about your great adventure, Magnolia. And your hero, Jess. Nice to meet you."

"Well," Magnolia looked at Jess, "I guess the only one left to introduce you to is Howard," who was standing there with his arm around Lisa, "Lisa's fiancé. He's the owner of the company we all work for. Well, if you can call what we do work."

"I am especially in your debt, Jess, thank you. I don't know what we would have done if anything bad had happened to Lisa's and, my soon to be, little sister," Howard said.

"So how is that book coming? The one that took you away from us and put you out on the high seas?" Lisa asked.

"Just before the storm caught up to me, I finished writing it. That's why I put it in the dry box, to keep it safe. And I made all of you villains and bullies in it. Except for my Lisa. I could never even pretend anything bad about you." Magnolia took her sister's hand.

"I think we better let our little novelist get some rest. Visiting hours are about to end anyway. We will see you tomorrow," Lisa said then she kissed Magnolia on the head and whispered, "Jess huh? We'll talk tomorrow."

"Yes, we will," Magnolia laughed.

After everyone left the room, Jess sat back down by Magnolia. "I am going, too. You need your rest and I need to go pick somethings up for us. You know, toothbrush for me, hairbrush for you, those sort of things. I'll be back the first thing in the morning." He kissed her hand and she smiled. "I love you, Magnolia."

"I love you, too, Jess," she said in an extremely sleepy voice. Jess stood up and walked to the door. He just stayed there, looking at her until she fell asleep, and then he left.

The next morning couldn't come fast enough for Jess. He was at the hospital as soon as visiting hours began. He came into Magnolia's room carrying boxes and bags.

"What's all this?" Magnolia asked, sitting up in bed.

"Just a few things no girl can live without," he handed the gifts to Magnolia and she opened them one by one.

"You bought me a nightgown and robe? Oh, Jess. You shouldn't have done that. I am just fine in the hospital gown."

"You are too beautiful to sit around in an old hospital gown. I want you to feel as beautiful as you look," Jess said. "Here. Open this one next."

She opened the next box, "Slippers!" she laughed.

The next few boxes contained items she could truly use during her recovery time in the hospital. A box of toiletries, a hairdryer, hairbrush, magazines; all intended to take her mind off the pain.

"Really, Jess? A new sundress. You have spent way too much money on me," Magnolia said.

"You have to have something to wear when you leave the hospital. I can't bring you anything from the island," Jess insisted.

"Why not? Aren't you coming back to see me?" Magnolia was afraid to hear his answer.

"No, I'm not coming back because I'm not leaving you, Magnolia. Not ever. That is if you will allow me...to marry you," Jess pulled the last box out of his pocket. He opened it up showing Magnolia the most beautiful ring she had ever seen.

"Oh Jess," she cried.

"Well...will you marry me?" Jess dropped to his knee and slid the ring on her finger.

"Yes! Yes! Yes! I will marry you! I love you, Jess," Magnolia had tears streaming down her face as Jess sat on the bed beside her.

Just at that moment the door to her room opened. Lisa walked in and saw her little sister crying. "What's happened? What's wrong?" Lisa ran to the bed.

"Nothing is wrong. Everything is perfect. Just perfect," Magnolia said holding up her hand showing Lisa her beautiful ring.

"Congratulations to you both!" Lisa almost yelled as she hugged her, soon to be, brother-in-law and gently hugged her sister.

"Can anyone join this party?" the doctor walked through the door and heard them talking.

"We have great news!" Jess said as Magnolia held her hand up again. "This beautiful young lady has agreed to be my bride."

"Well, congratulations! And I have more good news for you, Magnolia. If you follow doctor's orders and continue to improve, I will be releasing you in a day or two."

"That's wonderful, doctor," Lisa said.

"Thank you, doctor," Jess said.

Magnolia smiled and the doctor left. "Jess, where will I go? I don't want to go home with Lisa. No offense, Lisa. But it's too far from Jess. And I don't think I should stay on the island until we are married. Married! I love that word!"

"Don't worry. I have everything taken care of. I wasn't just shopping after I left you last night. I reserved two suites in the hotel down the street for us. We will stay there until you are better or until we are married. How does that sound to you?"

"Jess, it's too much. I love that you want to take care of me, but it's all too expensive. You just can't—" as she was speaking Lisa interrupted her.

She leaned down close to her sister and whispered, "Yes, he can." Lisa smiled at Jess, "I googled you, world famous artist."

Jess just shook his head, "There is that. I try to stay off the grid but I can't seem to manage."

"What are you two talking about?" Magnolia insisted.

"We are talking about what your Jess has failed to tell you. He has money, a lot of money. Like one of the richest men in America, kind of money," Lisa told her sister. "And he's marrying my little sister! I will never have to worry about you again!"

"Is that true?" Magnolia asked Jess.

"Does it make a difference, if I'm rich or poor? Would you love me either way?" Jess asked.

"I already do," Magnolia answered as she looked at her ring. "It's the most beautiful ring I've ever seen."

"That's exactly what my great-grandmother said when my great-grandfather slid it on her finger," Jess said as he looked at Magnolia. "I had it in a safe deposit box at the bank. For a long time, I thought it would be there forever. But now, it's on a hand that deserves its beauty." He kissed her hand.

"So, tell me, little sis. Where are you two having your wedding?" Lisa asked.

"Well, we haven't talked about it," Magnolia said as she looked at Jess.

"It's up to you. I will take you, and your family and friends, anywhere in the world to marry you," Jess told her.

"Anywhere in the world? Really?" Magnolia asked.

"Yes! Anywhere! You just name it," Jess answered her.

"Then, I would like to get married on your beach, at your lighthouse, with all these people, my family, with us," Magnolia said.

"You mean, our beach and our lighthouse. Are you sure?" Jess asked her.

"Absolutely! It's my favorite place in the whole world. I can't think of any place I would rather be when I marry the man I love," Magnolia said.

"I can't think of any place I would rather be when I marry the woman of my dreams," Jess leaned over to Magnolia and kissed her.

Lisa said, "Magnolia, you are absolutely glowing! Now tell your big sister, what kind of wedding do you want?"

Magnolia looked at her and said, "Glowing. I want my wedding to glow."

"Then that's what you will have," Jess said.

Chapter 16

"The Wedding"

As the ferry boat sped across the ocean toward Jess' island, Magnolia stood on the bow. Lisa walked up beside her, "Are you sure, Magnolia? Are you really sure that Jess is the one you want to marry?"

"Lisa," Magnolia hugged her sister, "you asked me this same question three months ago, when I was in the hospital. You asked me again when we were shopping for my wedding dress. The answer is the same today as it was both of those times, yes. I love Jess and I want to marry him."

Lisa put her arm around her little sister just as the ferry docked. Jess was waiting there to greet everyone. The captain threw him the rope, and he tied off the boat.

The first to step off the ferry was Jess' beautiful, bride to be. "Welcome home," Jess said to Magnolia, taking her hand as she stepped onto the dock.

"Oh, how I have missed this island!" Magnolia said as she drew a deep breath and looked around.

"So, this is where it all began," Lisa said. "What a fairytale romance you have had, little sister!"

"With a fairytale wedding to add to it," Kelly said.

After the wedding party and all their luggage were safely ashore, Jess shook the ferry captain's hand. "See you at 10:00," Jess said.

"Yes sir. I'll be back to pick up the wedding party and return them to the mainland," the captain said as he climbed back aboard. Jess untied the ropes and tossed them back onto the boat.

"Are you sure this is where you want to spend your honeymoon?" Jess asked Magnolia.

"There is nowhere in the world I would rather be than here on this island with you, Jess," Magnolia smiled at him.

"Well, let's get going. We have a wedding to attend," Jess laughed. "We will set the women up in the lighthouse and the men will be in the keeper's house." Adam, Tom, Howard, and Jess picked up all the luggage and started walking up the beach.

Lisa and Kelly followed, with Magnolia pointing out all her favorite places. When they got to the lighthouse, the men took all the suitcases in.

Jess and Magnolia stayed outside on the deck. He took her hands in his, "My beautiful Magnolia, will you marry me?"

"Jess, I already said yes. I'm wearing your ring. Of course, I'll marry you. Why do you ask me again?" Magnolia asked him.

"Because the first time I asked, you were lying in a hospital bed, in pain. That was not very romantic. But now, here we are, in the exact place where we met! We are standing by the rail where I grabbed your hand and pulled you over. The exact spot where my life began. I will ask you one more time. My Magnolia, will you marry me?"

"Oh yes! My love, Jess, I will marry you!" Magnolia had tears streaming down her face, her heart was pounding so hard she could barely breathe. This was the most romantic moment of her life.

At that second, the rest of the friends came out of the lighthouse. "Save some of those tears for the actual wedding," Adam said. "You know I'm the one performing the ceremony. You might need them."

Everyone laughed and Tom said, "Well, I guess we better let these ladies alone. I'm sure they have a lot of wedding things to do."

"So do we, come to think of it," Howard said looking over at all the garment bags they had carried with them.

"See you in a couple of hours," Jess said to Magnolia. As the men headed off to the keeper's house, Kelly, Lisa, and Magnolia went inside the lighthouse and shut the front door.

"Oh Magnolia! What a dream this is!" Kelly said, spinning around to look at everything at once.

"Oh! No! Let's make this very clear. This is not a dream. This is reality. My reality and Jess' reality," Magnolia laughed.

"Speaking of dreams, where is the painting?" Lisa asked her sister.

"It's in here," Magnolia opened the door to the lighthouse stairs.

Lisa looked in. "The drawings, the painting— they are... incredible!" Lisa was astonished, "I mean, I know he is a world-famous artist, but I never realized his work was so realistic. And that's when he first saw you."

"And fell in love with her," Kelly added. "What a story to tell your children and grandchildren! Then to wash up on his beach! This is the next book you should write, Magnolia. Your own love story."

Lisa hugged her little sister, "I'm so happy for you!"

"Oh, Lisa, Kelly, I am so happy!" Magnolia started to cry again.

"Let's stop that now, or we will all have red, swollen, eyes for the wedding," Lisa said.

"The wedding!" Lisa exclaimed, "We better get busy!"

At the keeper's house, the men were opening their garment bags and laying out their clothes. "I'm so glad you didn't go with tuxedoes for the wedding, Jess," Tom said.

"It's so hot on the beach here, we would swelter in full tuxes."

"Once the sun starts to set, it cools down fast by the ocean. I know that Magnolia doesn't care for anything too fancy and I wanted to keep with her style. Besides, who wants to wear a hot tuxedo anyway," Jess laughed.

"How do you plan to pull off the whole 'set up the wedding' thing?" Adam asked. "The beach looked pretty bare when we got here."

"What Magnolia doesn't know, is that, as the ferry was pulling away from our dock, another boat was speeding toward our island. That one carried the caterer, the staff and all the set up equipment," Jess said. "When Lisa asked Magnolia what kind of wedding she wanted, all she said was, 'glowing.' So, that's what she is going to have, a beach wedding, at sunset, that absolutely glows, with the moon glistening off the ocean in the background."

As the sun began its nightly drop from the sky, the men started their walk to pick up the ladies from the lighthouse. Each of them wore khaki pants with the cuffs slightly rolled up and white buttoned down shirts. When they reached the lighthouse, Adam walked up the steps and knocked on the door.

It soon opened with Kelly stepping out. She wore a knee-length, pink chiffon, strappy dress and carried a bouquet with pink lilies. She walked down the steps and Tom took her hand, "Stunning!" Tom said as they stepped aside.

Next, Lisa came out wearing a tea-length, pink, short-sleeved dress with a white netting overlay. She carried a bouquet that matched Kelly's. Lisa took Howard's arm as they walked over beside Tom and Kelly.

Jess was wringing his hands as he waited. "Calm down," Howard said, "It's not like she's going anywhere." Jess looked at him and laughed then he heard Adam clear his throat.

Jess looked up at the doorway and there stood the most breathtaking sight he had ever seen. His bride to be, his dream girl, his Magnolia. She wore her hair long, flowing and wavy, with a wreath of baby's breath around her head. Her white dress was made of fine lace with a silk underlining. It was a simple, sleeveless, A-lined dress that swept across the top of her bare feet. She held in her hand a bouquet of lilies and baby's breath.

Jess ran up the steps to meet her. She took his hand and they slowly walked down the steps. At the bottom, Jess stopped and turned to his love and said, "I love you. I hope it will be all you have ever dreamed."

"I love you, too, Jess. And it already is," Magnolia smiled at him.

Adam shut the lighthouse door and came bounding down the steps. "If everyone is ready, I think we have a wedding waiting for us on the beach," he said.

Jess and Magnolia walked just ahead of the others. The sun was just setting as they topped the sand dunes. Magnolia and Jess stopped walking and just stood with their bare feet in the warm sand, feeling the cool breeze blowing against them. The rest of the group came up behind them and kicked off their flip-flops to be bare foot like the bride and groom.

"Incredible!" Lisa said.

"Breathtaking!" Kelly said.

"Boy, you really pulled this one off," Adam said as he slapped Jess on the back.

The beach was lined with lanterns that glowed from their light. A long table was set with crystal and fine china. A small round table held the three-tiered wedding cake. Both tables were decorated with lace tablecloths and baby's breath flowers.

"Jess! It's glowing!" Magnolia said.

"So are you," Jess took her hand and they walked down the beach.

Jess and Magnolia stood just out of the ocean's reach as they said their vows. Howard and Tom stood by Jess while Lisa and Kelly stood beside Magnolia as Adam pronounced them, "husband and wife." As Jess kissed his bride, the tide rushed in over their feet. The rest of the group laughed and ran up out of the surf, but the freshly married couple didn't seem to notice... or care.

Immediately music began to play over the very well hidden speakers. "May I have this dance?" Jess asked Magnolia.

"You certainly may," Magnolia answered as she and Jess walked just far enough up the beach to be out of the incoming tide. He reached out and took her hand to dance.

Jess pulled her in close to him as Magnolia's favorite song began to play. He, very quietly, sang to her, "Looking back on the memory of the dance we shared beneath the stars above..."

Tom looked at Kelly, "That's a rather strange choice for a 'first dance' song, Garth Brooks' 'The Dance'."

"It's her favorite song. That's why he chose it," Kelly replied.

Lisa had tears streaming down her face as she watched her little sister and new brother sway together with the moon rising over the ocean behind them.

"She's happy," Howard said to Lisa. "I hope someday, I can make you that happy." Lisa just smiled and laid her head on his shoulder.

At the end of the song, Magnolia looked at Jess and said, "You read my book."

"Yes, I did. And I loved it! Now, let's dance," he said as the next song came on. The other couples came over and joined in the dancing.

Soon everyone was hungry and thirsty. As they sat down at the table to eat, waiters appeared from, seemingly, out of nowhere. They catered to the needs of everyone in the wedding party. Even the photographer, who had been taking pictures from afar, was now apparent.

"Where did they all come from?" Magnolia asked.

"You said you only wanted those you consider to be family at our wedding, so that's what we had. But the reception is a different story," Jess laughed.

"Wonderful!" Magnolia said as she lifted her glass to be filled with champagne.

After eating and dancing and cutting the cake, it was time for the ferry to return the wedding party to the mainland. Magnolia and Jess stood on the dock and hugged everyone goodbye. Then, she and Jess walked back to the sand. As the ferry pulled away, shouts of, "We love you, we'll miss you," were heard as Magnolia waved.

As the full moon reached the top of the sky, the ocean glistened from its light. Magnolia looked back at the lanterns that were still burning up and down the beach. "Everything was perfect, Jess. This has been the happiest day of my life," Magnolia said.

"It's only the beginning my love," Jess said as he put his arm around her for their walk back to the lighthouse, "only the beginning."

END